# I Can Choose
# My Bedtime Story

**\* \* \* \* \* \* \* \* \* \* \* \* \* \* \* \* \* \* \* \* \* \***

# I Can Choose My Bedtime Story

Edited by Mary Parsley · Illustrations by Claude Kaïler and Rosemary Lowndes

Grosset & Dunlap · Publishers · New York

**\* \* \* \* \* \* \* \* \* \* \* \* \* \* \* \* \* \* \* \* \* \***

# List of Stories

Copyright © Eurobook Limited, 1971
Designed and produced for the Publisher by
Eurobook Limited, London.

Published in the United States by Grosset &
Dunlap, Inc.
All rights reserved.
Printed in the United States of America.
1977 PRINTING

ISBN: 0-448-02820-4 (Trade)
ISBN: 0-448-13362-8 (Library)
Library of Congress Catalog Card Number:
77-152557

# Introduction

What shall the bedtime story be tonight? There are so many to choose from! Will it be about a

or a

The pictorial title pages of this book, like its cover, are especially designed for children who are too young to read. They can now participate in the bedtime story in a very important way— by choosing a picture, they choose the story they would like to hear. There is one picture for each story, and the page number in the corner tells you where to find it.

The stories are all written to be read aloud (often with sound effects!), and it is hoped that the parent will enjoy them as much as the child does. The illustrations are delightful with or without the stories and will provide food for young imaginations at any time of the day.

Is a funny story wanted? Then read about the

who had hiccups or the sheep who went to school. Or how about an adventure in a helicopter or a game of

There are 54 stories about all sorts of different things—a wonderful variety for every child to choose from.

Mary Parsley

# Bartholomew the Beach Donkey

Bartholomew was a beach donkey. For a nickle a time, and a dime on Sundays, he gave children rides up and down the beach every day of the summer. As soon as it was light he would be taken down to the beach and he would stay there, giving rides to the children, until the sun dropped beneath the sea. Bartholomew was very happy in the summer. He loved the children with their gay chatter, and the fat gentlemen in deckchairs with newspapers over their heads, and the jolly ladies whose legs turned pink in the sun.

Bartholomew wished that summer would go on for ever and ever, but it never did. Suddenly one day in late September he would know that it was over. He would come down to the beach and there would be only a handful of deckchairs set out. The children would be fewer and their mothers and fathers would be wearing sweaters to keep off the cool wind that was blowing from the sea. The Punch and Judy man had already packed up his show for the winter, and the big

ferris wheel on the fairground was standing still and silent. In a few days there would be nobody there at all, and that was when Bartholomew started to feel really miserable. He would wander up and down the deserted beach, and there would be nobody to talk to except the crabs, who didn't have much to say at all, and the seagulls, who talked much too much and always complained about how hungry they were.

One particularly bleak winter's day, when there were dark clouds over the cliffs and the sea looked grey and angry, Bartholomew was standing in the middle of the empty beach shivering with cold and wishing desperately that the spring would hurry up.

"Brrrr," he shuddered, "how I hate the winter!"

"Winter?" said a voice. "So that's what you call it."

Bartholomew looked around to see who was speaking. There, jumping up and down in the waves at the sea's edge, was a large fish with a smiling face. It was a dolphin.

"Goodness, who are you?" said Bartholomew. He had never seen a dolphin before.

"I'm a dolphin," said the dolphin, "and I had never heard of winter till you mentioned it. You see, I'm terribly lost. I took the wrong turn somewhere far out in the ocean, and I've ended up here."

"What do you mean, you've never heard of winter?" said Bartholomew.

"Well, I come from a place where there is no winter," said the dolphin. "There are warm seas and palm trees and soft golden beaches and great big turtles who play with us in the surf. I had never known what it was like to feel cold till I came here."

Bartholomew opened his eyes in wonder.

"Gosh, how wonderful!" he said. "A place where it is summer all the year! How I wish I could go there!"

"Yes, it is pretty nice," said the dolphin, "and right now I wish I were back there. I think I had better turn around and see if I can find my way home."

"Oh, don't go just yet," pleaded Bartholomew. "Tell me some more about your warm seas and your hot summer days. Then I can think about it during the winter, and pretend I am there. That way I won't feel quite so cold and miserable."

So the dolphin stayed a while longer and told Bartholomew all he could think of about where he lived. And when at last he waved goodbye and disappeared out to sea again, Bartholomew imagined this lovely summery place and he began to feel a warm glow on his back as though he were really there with the sun shining down from a brilliant blue sky. Every day of that winter he thought about it, and that way he didn't notice so much the cold wind and the rain that blew down on to his lonely beach.

Soon the summer was back again, and the deckchairs and the Punch and Judy man, and the laughing children who wanted rides on his back.

"How wonderful that the summer is here," thought Bartholomew. "It is like a new life every time it comes around again." And then he thought that perhaps it was better to stay here after all, because even if the winter was cold and wet, it was good to have the summer to look forward to.

# The Castle Robber

There was once a king who lived in a beautiful castle with his beautiful little daughter, Princess Scilla.

One day a wicked man named Hugo came to the castle. No one knew he was wicked, but he was, as you shall soon see. He told the King a pack of lies and the King, poor fellow, believed him.

"A band of robbers is hiding in the mountains," cried wicked Hugo. "They are going to come here and rob your castle!"

"What shall I do?" gasped the King.

"Go to the mountains. Catch them by surprise and chase them away," said Hugo.

"How clever you are," said the King, not knowing what a clever *liar* Hugo was!

But then the King began to worry. "Who will look after my daughter and my castle while I'm away?" he asked.

"Well, I suppose I could stay and look after them," said wicked Hugo. He pretended he wasn't very anxious to stay. But of course, it was just what he wanted, as you shall soon see.

The King begged him to stay and guard the princess. So wicked Hugo agreed. But he laughed to himself, thinking of his wicked plans.

The King called for Princess Scilla. "This good man," he said, pointing to Hugo, "will take care of you while I'm away."

Princess Scilla didn't like Hugo. She didn't know he was wicked, but she didn't like him. Her little dog, David, growled and barked. He didn't like Hugo either.

Princess Scilla was frightened. "Let me come with you, Father," she cried.

But the King wouldn't take her. He was sure she would be safe with Hugo!

He called his men from the castle. Each one carried a big stick for fighting. The King, being a king, had the biggest fighting stick. He climbed on his horse, called to his men, waved goodbye to the princess, and hurried to the mountains.

No sooner was he gone, than Hugo showed what a wicked man he was! He caught Princess Scilla and locked her in the tower! She ran to the window and called for help.

The cook heard her cries, and ran to let her out. Hugo caught the cook and locked her in the tower, too! So they both called for help. Others came to let them out, but Hugo caught them, too! Soon every girl and woman was locked in the tower, shrieking and shouting for help.

Wicked Hugo laughed. "All the men have gone to catch robbers, so there's no one to help you," he said. "And the joke is, there *aren't* any robbers. Except me!"

Then he took the King's crown, and grabbed all the King's money-bags, and stole all the King's treasure. He ran away, leaving the princess and the womenfolk wailing and lamenting in the tower!

It seemed he'd got clear away with his wicked robbery. But he forgot about Princess Scilla's little dog, David.

For, when David saw Hugo locking everyone in the tower, he ran to the mountains. He soon found the King and his men. They were very puzzled because they had found no robbers, nor any sign of robbers.

David couldn't *say* what was wrong, but he barked and howled and jumped about, and the King soon understood him.

"Back to the castle!" he cried. "Something is wrong there!"

He charged away on his great horse, with all the men running behind. And when he reached the castle, what did he see? He saw wicked Hugo creeping out of the gate with a great sack of loot!

The King gave Hugo a great whack with his stick. Then he galloped straight into the castle. He unlocked the tower and rescued the princess and the womenfolk.

After that one good whack from the King's stick, Hugo dropped his loot and ran. Right behind him chased all the men, and every one of them gave Hugo a whack with his stick. He ran right out of the kingdom and never returned.

The little dog David was the hero of the day. Princess Scilla gave him a big kiss. The King gave him a big medal. The cook gave him a big meal. And they all lived happily ever after.

# The Clever Panda

In the high, wild hills of northern China lived a big, fat panda. Part of his fur was white, and part of it was black. His head was white, and he had big black circles around his eyes. He lived alone, wandering through the hills, but he wasn't lonely. He liked being alone.

One day, two hunters came to the hills with their dogs. They wanted to catch a panda and take him to their zoo, where everyone could see him. That would be very nice for the people, because everyone likes to see a panda. But *he* wouldn't like it.

The hunters saw the panda and chased after him. He ran into a bamboo thicket, so they couldn't see him. Then he ran until he couldn't hear them any more.

After his long run, he was very hungry. So he sat down and began eating juicy bamboo shoots, his favorite food.

The hunters' dogs crept silently along the panda's trail. They surrounded him, and suddenly leaped from the thicket! He just sat looking at them, very surprised, like an overgrown cuddly toy.

"Yap, yap, yap!" called the dogs, feeling very brave. They weren't afraid of a toy, no matter how big he was.

The panda dropped his bamboo shoot. He jumped at the dogs and waved his big sharp claws under their noses. He opened his big mouth and showed them all his big strong teeth. He growled a big growl. "Scat, you silly dogs!" he bellowed.

My, those dogs were scared! They yipped and yapped and howled and ran. They ran till they couldn't run any more, and they never went near a panda again.

The panda laughed. He wouldn't ever hurt the dogs, but *they* didn't know that.

"After all the excitement I feel quite hungry again," said the panda. So he sat down to eat some more bamboo. He forgot all about the two hunters.

He made so much noise, chomping and

chewing his food, he couldn't hear anything else. The hunters crept close. Then they jumped from the thicket and threw a net over him. Before he could say "Himalayas", the panda was caught in the net!

The hunters smiled at him. "Don't worry, we won't hurt you," they said. "We only want to take you to the zoo, where you'll never be cold or lonely again. We'll feed you on honey and oats and fresh fruit and all kinds of lovely food. You'll like it."

"Humph! I'm sure I won't like it at all," grumbled the panda. "I never feel cold, because I have a thick fur coat. I never feel lonely, because I like being alone. And I don't want all your fancy food. I like bamboo better than anything. Please let me go."

"No, no!" said the hunters. "We've caught you, and you're coming to the zoo!"

They tied the net to a pole and started down the hill, carrying the panda all wrapped up in the net.

The panda lay still. He didn't struggle. He was busy thinking. At last he thought of a way to escape. He began to moan and groan. "Ohhh, I'm so hungry," he wailed.

"Wait till we reach the zoo," said the hunters. "We'll feed you there."

"I'm too hungry," sobbed the panda.

The hunters stopped. They cut lots of bamboo shoots and pushed them through the holes in the net for the panda. Then they picked him up and went on. He was heavy, and they began to feel very tired.

They were so tired, they didn't notice what the clever panda was doing. He lay in the net, chomping happily. They thought he was eating the bamboo. He wasn't. He was chewing a hole in the net. Suddenly, with a scramble and a leap, he was out of the net. He ran up the hill.

The hunters were too tired to chase him. "Stop! Come back!" they called. "Don't you want to come to our lovely zoo?"

The panda laughed, with a big, happy, panda kind of laugh. "Ho, ho," he shouted down at them. "If your zoo's so wonderful, why don't *you* go and live in it?"

He disappeared up the hill, laughing like anything. "Thanks for the ride!" he called. And that was the last they ever saw or heard of the clever panda.

# The Yetis' New Home

Once, long ago, there was a yeti called Khan. In those days the yetis – who are a kind of large ape – lived in the deep valleys of Nepal. All around towered the great snowy Himalaya mountains, but in the valleys, in summer, it was warm and sunny and the farmers grew pineapples and bananas and rice.

But the farmers didn't like yetis, even though the yetis tried hard to be friendly. They were just too different. "All you yetis do is sleep all day and eat all night," the farmers complained. "You don't work for a living the way we have to. You just enjoy yourselves eating what *we* grow without paying for it."

"But we don't eat very much," the yetis said, "and anyway, we lived in Nepal before you did!"

"Who cares?" replied the farmers. "You are in the way. You'll have to go. From now on if we catch any of you on our farms again we will kill you."

Well, there were many more farmers than yetis, so there was nothing else for the yetis to do but find somewhere else to live.

This was where Khan took over, because he was the strongest, cleverest yeti of them all. So if anyone could find them a new home – somewhere safe and far away from all farmers – he could.

Khan set out. First he went south to the great plains of India. But there were many,

many farms and farmers there. Then he went east – but here again he found lots of people. So next he searched in the west, but here he found only empty desert, hot and dry.

At last, only the north remained, where the great Himalayas were at their highest, reaching above the clouds so high that there were no trees and the snow lasted all the year round. Even lower down there was hardly anything to eat, and the only places Khan could find to live were some big caves – cold, and dark, and miserable.

When the other yetis saw the caves, it was their turn to grumble. "What shall we eat?" they said. "There are no bananas here, no pineapples, no rice!"

"No, and no farmers either," cried Khan. "Friends, to the east there are farmers, to the west there are farmers, and to the south there are still more farmers. I have searched everywhere, and this is the only place left for us to go."

"But whatever shall we eat?" asked one of the other yetis.

"We must collect what we can during the summer," said Khan. "There are some little plants, and grass and moss. And if we are very careful we can still get some food from the valleys – but we must stay hidden and never let the farmers catch us."

And so the yetis went to live in the mountains. They grew lots of long hair on their bodies to keep themselves warm and they stayed in their caves all through the winters, only coming out – at night – in the spring and summer.

In the valleys the farmers weren't quite as pleased to get rid of the yetis as they thought they were going to be. They became rather ashamed of themselves, and some of them began to leave food outside their doors every night for the yetis to find.

They still do. But the yetis have never tried to make friends with the farmers again. Instead they have hidden themselves in their caves so carefully, and for so long, that now nobody can remember what a yeti looks like. And there are some people who don't even believe they exist at all.

But just you ask the farmers of Nepal!

# Francis Ferret Stays at Home

Francis Ferret was having an argument with his friend Reggie Squirrel. They were sitting down for tea in Francis Ferret's house.

"I'm cleverer than you," said Reggie Squirrel. "Of course I am."

"No, you are *not*," said Francis Ferret.

"I bet I am," said Reggie.

"Prove it, then," said Francis. He said it mainly to stop the argument. It really didn't matter at all, but Reggie kept at it.

"All right," said Reggie. "I bet I can make you step outside your house. If you step outside your house tomorrow, that will prove I'm cleverer than you."

Francis Ferret smiled. All he had to do was stay at home tomorrow. It was too easy.

They agreed that Reggie himself was not allowed inside the house. Nor was he to do anything dangerous. Then Reggie Squirrel went home.

The next day Francis Ferret was having his breakfast when there was a knock at the door.

Francis opened the door. There on his doorstep stood a funny-looking man. He wore a long driving coat, a cloth cap and big round driving goggles which covered his eyes.

"Excuse me," said the man. "My car's broken down. It's just down the road. I wonder if you could come and have a look at it for me."

"Oh, yes. Certainly," said Francis Ferret, who liked to help people if he could. He was just about to step outside the house when he noticed something odd about the man. From his back there grew a long grey bushy tail.

"Ah, I'm sorry, Reggie Squirrel," said Francis. "I've just remembered that I don't know anything about cars."

With that, Francis shut his door. Then he laughed and laughed at Reggie Squirrel in his driving coat.

Francis was still laughing when he heard

a strange noise in the chimney. A sort of fluttering noise. Then a voice said:

"Coo coo. Coo coo. Can you help me, please?"

Francis looked into his fireplace.

"Who is it?" he asked.

"Coo coo. I'm a pigeon and I'm stuck in your chimney. Coo coo. Please help."

"Wait a moment," said Francis. "I'll pull you out."

Francis was about to run outside to climb on to the roof when he noticed a ladder leaning against the wall, just outside his window. Someone had already climbed on to the roof.

"I'll fix that Reggie Squirrel," said Francis. He leaned out of the window and pushed the ladder away from the wall. It fell to the ground with a great clatter. Francis went back to his fireplace.

"Coo coo. Coo coo, Reggie Squirrel," called Francis Ferret. "Now you're stuck on my roof. Coo coo."

"Hey, put that ladder back," cried Reggie Squirrel down the chimney. "That's not fair. Oooh! Ow!"

There was a tremendous crashing noise in the chimney. Soot poured into the room and then, with a cry and a bump, Reggie Squirrel landed in the fireplace. His face was black with soot.

"I slipped," said Reggie.

Francis Ferret roared with laughter at the unlucky Reggie. Then he went outside to fetch a bucket of water to clean up his friend. But when he came back Reggie shouted:

"There! That proves it. I made you step outside your house to fetch the water. That proves I'm cleverer than you."

Reggie looked much happier in spite of the soot on his face.

Then Francis Ferret said, "Yes. But you aren't allowed inside my house today. That was one of the rules."

Reggie had not thought of that. He looked disappointed and began to shake soot all over the room.

"I'll tell you what," said Francis. "Let's say we're equally clever."

Reggie Squirrel's eyes grew bright.

"All right," he said. "Let's say we're equally clever."

# Scratchy Spider
# and the Eight Cream Buns

Scratchy Spider was a villain. He stole cream buns from ladies' shopping bags. He crept up behind them. Then, with one spidery leg, he grabbed a cream bun and made off.

Scratchy Spider was very fast and no one had ever been able to catch him. He ran and quickly hid himself in a crowd. Or else he climbed a wall or jumped from one building to another. By the time the police arrived, Scratchy Spider had always vanished. And no one knew where Scratchy Spider lived.

Scratchy Spider had twelve legs altogether. He didn't need them all for running away. If he used one spidery leg to grab a cream bun, he still had eleven spidery legs to use for running away. If he stole two cream buns, he could still escape on the other ten legs. And so on.

But Scratchy Spider was greedy. He wanted more and more cream buns. Each day he lined up the cream buns he had taken. Then, before he ate them, he counted them. He was never satisfied.

"It's not enough," said Scratchy Spider. "I must have more cream buns."

One day he was in a tremendously greedy mood. Suddenly he said:

"Tomorrow I will steal eight cream buns at once!"

It was a crazy idea. The most he had ever stolen at one time was four. Eight cream buns would make a heavy load. He would need eight legs to carry them and that left only four legs to use for running away. It was a mad plan but Scratchy was wild and greedy for cream buns.

The next day he went to a busy street. He waited until there were plenty of ladies with cream buns in their shopping bags. He

looked most of all for ladies with large, heavy shopping bags. They could not run so fast.

Scratchy Spider's big moment arrived. Along the street he counted eight ladies. They had all bought cream buns and they all carried heavy shopping bags.

Scratchy Spider struck. He ran alongside the first lady. Snatch! Before the lady could stop him Scratchy Spider was dealing with the next lady. Snatch! Two cream buns were clasped in two spidery legs.

So it went on. Snatch! Snatch! Snatch! Five cream buns – the most he had ever stolen at one time. Snatch! Six.

Six cream buns made a heavy load, but Scratchy Spider was greedy for more. Snatch! Seven. Now for the last one. He ran up behind the eighth lady. Snatch! Eight spidery legs with a cream bun in each. It was a most unusual sight.

The eight ladies all screamed and ran after Scratchy Spider. He ran faster than they could but the eight cream buns made a heavy load. And he was not used to running on only four legs.

Away went Scratchy Spider. But he couldn't lose the eight ladies. They still carried their heavy shopping bags and couldn't quite catch up with the greedy spider. Nor could Scratchy outrun the ladies.

They raced along for a quarter of a mile. Everyone was out of breath. Then the biggest of the eight ladies stopped. She put down her heavy shopping bag.

"I'll get him," she called to the other seven ladies. They were all so tired that they stopped as well.

The Big Lady pulled a great long loaf of French bread from her shopping bag.

"Now we'll see," she said. She drew back her arm and threw the French loaf as hard as she could.

The French loaf whirled and twisted in the air. But the Big Lady's aim was good and the loaf went straight for Scratchy Spider. It caught him fair and square.

Scratchy Spider gave a shriek of surprise as his legs disappeared from under him.

"Quick, ladies," called the Big Lady. And before Scratchy Spider could move, the eight ladies tied him in a neat bundle and handed him over to the police.

Scratchy Spider was sent away to a place where he could only have cream buns twice a week. After a few weeks of that, he learned to like other foods as well, and became a quieter, more likeable spider.

# Brendan the Owl

Brendan the Owl lived in the town park, in a large weeping willow tree.

One morning some children were playing near the tree when they saw a sign pointing to Brendan's house. The sign said: TO THE OWL.

The children stepped through the long trailing branches of the weeping willow to find the owl.

Inside the great dome of the willow tree it was cool and quiet. Small rays of sunlight came through the upper branches and shone here and there on the faces of the children.

"Hello, Owl," they called, looking up at Brendan's house. There was no reply.

"Hello. Hello, Owl," they called again. Silence.

"Owl," cried the children, their voices growing louder. "Are you there, Owl?"

No reply. No owl. Feeling rather sad, the children turned to go. Then:

"Of course I'm here," croaked a small weary voice.

The children looked up. There, at the door of his tree-trunk house, blinking down at them through half-closed sleepy eyes, and still tying the cord of a bright blue dressing-gown, stood Brendan the Owl.

"Oh," said the children, "we thought you were out somewhere."

"I was in all right," said Brendan. "I'm always in at this time. It's just that you've, you've . . ."

Brendan stopped talking and his beak began to open wider. It opened wider and wider until it would stretch no further. His upper beak pointed to the sky, his lower beak pointed down toward the children. It was one of the largest yawns Brendan had ever yawned. At the end of it he huffed and hooted for a full half-minute: "HOOOOO-WHOOOOOOOOOOOH!"

"I do beg your pardon," said Brendan when it was all over. He politely patted his beak with a wing.

"Of course!" said one of the children,

remembering at last. "Owls only come out at night. And we woke you up."

"Oh dear," said all the children together. "We're very sorry. We must let you go back to bed."

"That's all right," said Brendan. "It's nice to see you all. I haven't had a visitor for ages."

Fortunately he was an owl of even temper. All the same, he was rather sleepy.

"Look," said Brendan, "why don't we meet again later? I'll have a bit of a sleep as usual, and you can call for me at about half-past four."

Everyone thought that was a splendid idea. The children went home for lunch and Brendan, of course, climbed back into bed. Soon he was deeply asleep.

At exactly half-past four they met again. Brendan had put on a bright blue vest (blue was his favorite color and a dark blue cap with a long peak to keep the sun out of his eyes.

Then they went to the playground in the corner of the park, the children running and Brendan flapping his wings and flying just above their heads.

They played on the swings, the seesaw, and the long slide. Brendan liked the slide best of all, and hooted, "Whoo hooo, whoo hooo" each time he whizzed down it. They played and chased each other until the sun turned from red to orange and began to go down on the horizon.

"What a marvelous day I've had," said Brendan as he flew back to his tree.

"Goodbye, Brendan," called the children. "See you tomorrow."

And so they did. Every day they played together for the rest of the summer, racing and chasing all over the park.

Brendan soon became the most famous owl for miles around. When visitors came to see him, they found a bright new sign outside the weeping willow tree. It said, in large blue letters:

TO BRENDAN THE OWL
(AFTER 4:30, PLEASE).

# King John and the Abbot of Canterbury

This is a very old story about a very bad king called John. Whenever he was angry – which was most of the time – he would do cruel, unkind things. This made everybody hate him, which, of course, just made him angrier and more cruel than ever.

One day, when he was in an especially bad mood, he called the wise old Abbot of Canterbury to his throne room.

"Listen to me, old Abbot," said the King. "Everyone thinks you are very wise and very clever – but I don't. I don't think you are clever at all, and anyway you are far too old to be of any help to me."

The poor Abbot didn't know what to say, so he just bowed his head.

"So," went on King John, "to prove whether you are clever or stupid, I'm going to ask you a question. Just one. If you can answer it I will give you the richest gifts I can afford. . . ."

"And if I cannot answer it?" asked the Abbot.

"Why, then I shall have your head cut off," snarled the wicked King.

"What, then, is the question, Your Majesty?"

"*What do I think?*" replied the King, looking very pleased with himself.

"Oh dear, oh dear," gasped the poor old Abbot to himself. "How can I possibly know what the King is thinking?" Then out loud he said:

"Are you thinking about the crown?"

"No!" snarled King John.

"Are you thinking about the palace?"

"Wrong again," shouted the King.

"Then surely you are thinking about money?"

"NO! NO!! NO!!! you old fool," bellowed King John, trembling with rage. "OFF WITH HIS HEAD."

The poor old Abbot of Canterbury fell on his knees and begged for another chance. "Please, Your Majesty," he said. "If you give me some time to think I am sure I could get it right."

Well, of course, King John really wanted to have the Abbot's head chopped off. But he wanted him to suffer as much as possible, so he said:

"Very well, I'll give you one last chance. Come back in a week and try again. But if you don't get it right then – OFF WITH YOUR HEAD!"

So the Abbot went home to think. He thought all day for six days, and he thought all night for six days. He read piles of books. But none of it was any good. At the end of the week he was no nearer finding the answer than he had been at the beginning. But on the seventh and last day, as he was walking sadly through his garden, he met his old servant, the gardener.

"My lord Abbot, whatever is the matter? Why do you look sad?" the gardener asked.

"Ah, my old friend and servant. To-morrow I must tell the King what he thinks, or he will have my head cut off. And I have tried and *tried* to find an answer, but I haven't the faintest idea what to say. By this time tomorrow I will probably be dead!"

"Ho, ho, my lord of Canterbury," laughed the gardener, "you are very clever, but I see there are still some things even an old gardener can teach you. Don't you worry. Just lend me your robe and your sandals, and I'll tell the King what he thinks, have no fear."

So the next day the old gardener disguised himself as the Abbot and went to the palace. Boldly he marched up to King John.

"Your Majesty," he said, "I have come to answer your question!"

"Right, my fine Abbot of Canterbury," said King John, "WHAT DO I THINK?"

"Think – why, *you think I'm the Abbot of Canterbury*, that's what!" cried the old gardener. Then he pulled off the Abbot's brown robe and sandals, so the King could see it wasn't the Abbot at all. "But I'm only his poor servant, as you can see, so pardon him and pardon me!"

And do you know, there must have been some good in bad King John after all, because he did forgive the Abbot, and the old gardener, and gave them many rich presents too, to make up for his earlier wickedness.

# The Amazing Window-Washer

Professor Craze was excited. He was about to test the Sploshomatic. It was his newest invention.

For weeks the Professor had been building a machine that would wash and polish the windows of his house at an amazing speed. Now it was ready.

The main part of the Sploshomatic was a large green box. Inside the box was the motor. The box itself stood on two yellow rubber feet. On top of the motor there was a Revolving Eye (for finding windows) and two containers. One container was marked "Water" and a sign on the other said "Polish."

"Now, Sploshomatic," said the Professor, putting on his gardening gloves. "Let's see what you can do."

Professor Craze bent low over the controls and pressed the starter switch to "On." Now...

A green light shone in the Revolving Eye. A moment later it had spotted the Professor's kitchen windows. The machine padded softly toward the windows on its two yellow rubber feet.

When it reached the windows the Sploshomatic stopped. There was a loud buzzing noise. Two long thin arms came slowly out of the containers marked "Water" and "Polish."

On the end of the arm which had come from the container marked "Water" was a large sponge. The other arm held a big yellow duster which had been dipped in the Professor's special red polish.

Soon Professor Craze's kitchen windows were covered with water. Then the "Polish" arm began to swing sideways and back, sideways and back. In no time at all, the windows gleamed like new crystal.

"Wonderful!" cried the Professor. "It really works!" This was a very pleasant change for the Professor, as most of his machines failed to work at all.

Already the Sploshomatic was hard at work on the next window. SPLUSH SPLOSH SPLUSH SPLOSH, went the "Water" arm, SQUEAK RUB SQUEAK RUB, went the "Polish" arm. And very soon the job was done.

Now the Sploshomatic was going faster. The Green Eye noticed the Professor's bedroom on the upper floor of the house. In a flash the yellow rubber feet began to run up the wall of the house. SPLUSHER SPLOSHER, SQUEAKY RUB. And the job was done.

But now the machine was going too fast. Its long thin arms were waving about just anywhere. CRASH! The "Water" arm went right through a window.

"Stop! Stop!" shouted Professor Craze. He tried to catch the mad Sploshomatic. But it ran up the wall of the house again and broke the skylight on the roof. CRASH!

"I must stop it somehow," said the Professor to himself. He was very upset. CRASH! Another window was broken.

Quickly Professor Craze fetched a large barrel from his workshop. He filled it to the top with water, then carried it into the garden and placed it on the ground.

Up at the top of the house the Sploshomatic was still busy looking for windows. The Green Eye whizzed around and around. It glowed with a strange, dark light.

"Hey, Sploshomatic," called the Professor. He pointed to the water barrel. "Here's a window you forgot to clean."

The Green Eye of the Sploshomatic looked down. It saw the glassy surface of the water in the barrel. It looked just like a window.

The Green Eye grew darker. Then the Sploshomatic gave a great jump. It fell straight into the barrel and quickly spluttered to a stop.

"Thank goodness for that," said Professor Craze when it was all over. "What an ill-mannered machine. Breaking all my windows. I think I'll stick to inventing things that don't rush around quite so much."

And he went into his house to have a nice, quiet rest.

# The Colonel's Sausage

Martin lived in a small country town. In the town square stood a lucky fountain. When people wanted to bring good luck, they made a wish and threw a coin in the water. The floor of the fountain sparkled with coins of every color.

In the middle of the fountain was a stone statue. This was the statue of the Colonel. He had a three-cornered hat and long boots which reached above his knees. The Colonel had been a famous war hero many years ago.

One day Martin was walking alone by the fountain. He looked at the coins shining in the water. Then, from out of the air, came a sigh. A voice said:

"By my boots! That's a fine sausage."

Martin looked up. He was quite alone in the square. Except for the statue of the Colonel. Then he saw the stone lips of the statue begin to move.

"That shop," said the Colonel, "sells the most wonderful sausage."

Martin followed the way the Colonel's head was pointing. There, in the corner of the square, was a grocer's shop. Rows of different sausages, pink and grey and brown and black, hung in the window.

"Look, boy," said the Colonel. "Take some money out of my fountain, would you, and bring me a piece of that long pink sausage over there."

Martin was surprised but he did as the Colonel asked. When he came back from

"Buying sausage for the Colonel? I should say so."

Martin was very unhappy. Things looked bad for him. Then he had an idea.

As the sun went down Martin and the policeman stood in the corner of the square. They watched the statue of the Colonel. In the Colonel's hand was a new piece of sausage which Martin had put there. They waited and waited. The Colonel did not move. It grew dark and the moon shone over the square.

Then, suddenly, the Colonel's head bent forward. The hand holding the sausage flew to the Colonel's mouth. The hand fell back and the Colonel was still.

But the sausage had gone.

The next day Martin and the policeman went up to the statue. The Mayor of the town was with them.

"Now then, Colonel," said the policeman. "You can't go asking people to take coins from the fountain. It's not their money and it's not your money."

The Colonel's stone mouth opened.

"I'm sorry about the coins," said the Colonel. "But I get so hungry. I've been standing here for three hundred years, you know."

Martin felt sorry for the Colonel.

"Sir," he said to the Mayor. "Couldn't the town buy the Colonel a piece of sausage from time to time? After all, he does belong to the town."

The Mayor beamed. "That's a splendid idea, Martin," he cried. "I agree."

And from that day, Martin took the Colonel a piece of Town sausage every Tuesday afternoon. By Wednesday morning the sausage was always gone.

the shop, he placed the sausage in the Colonel's hand. The Colonel did not move or speak. Not even to say "thank you."

The next day Martin went to see the statue again. He waited in silence for almost ten minutes. Then the stone lips began to move.

"By my boots, boy," said the Colonel. "That was tasty sausage. Get me another piece, would you?"

The Colonel sounded pleased. Martin reached into the fountain for more coins. But as he did so, a new voice shouted:

"Aha! I should say so!"

Martin was pulled away from the fountain. There stood a large policeman.

"Come with me, boy," ordered the policeman, and he dragged Martin away to the police station.

"Now, boy," said the policeman. "Pinching coins from the fountain, eh? I should say so!"

Martin tried to explain. But the policeman shook his head.

# The Harvest Mouse

Jeremy Harvest Mouse lived on the edge of a wheatfield. He lived with his mother and father and his three brothers and two sisters. Jeremy was the youngest of the Harvest Mouse family.

During Jeremy's first summer their home was a round nest made from bits of grass and corn leaves. The nest had a door in the side, and the floor and walls were lined with flower petals and leaves.

One bright day, Jeremy's parents were out looking for food and his brothers and sisters were away visiting their friends in the next field. Jeremy decided to go for a walk in the wheatfield.

He stepped out of the nest and hopped off among the tall stalks of wheat. Like all the Harvest Mouse family, Jeremy was light enough and nimble enough to climb up the stalks and eat the ripe ears of wheat at the top. From time to time Jeremy helped himself to a few tasty mouthfuls of wheat.

The sun shone down on the field and Jeremy wandered further and further away from his nest. Until he wasn't quite sure where he was.

Then, at first in the distance but coming nearer, Jeremy heard a strange noise. The noise grew louder and louder. Soon the earth he was walking on began to shake, and the wheat ears began to tremble and rustle together.

Suddenly, with a huge crashing and thrashing, an enormous Red Monster with whirling blades thundered past not six feet from where Jeremy Harvest Mouse was standing. All the wheat which had been growing in the path of the Monster – had gone. Vanished. Only the stubby yellow feet were left.

Jeremy was frightened. "What shall I do?" he asked himself. Other small animals, fieldmice, rats and rabbits, were rushing about nearby. In the distance the Red Monster turned and came back. Now it was heading straight for Jeremy.

"What am I going to do?" thought Jeremy. "That Monster is cutting up the whole field. It'll cut me up if I don't look out."

Jeremy tried to ask a passing rabbit for advice. But the Rabbit hardly saw him.

"No time. No time," muttered the Rabbit and disappeared.

Then Jeremy noticed a rat standing next to him.

"Please, Rat . . ." began Jeremy.

"Take care," said the Rat, and dashed away through the wheat. Now the Red

Monster was coming closer. Great bundles of wheat were torn up and fed into its hungry, thrashing, crashing jaws.

The Red Monster was only ten feet away when Jeremy felt a tap on his back. It was another Harvest Mouse.

"Quick," said the Other Harvest Mouse. "In here." And he pushed Jeremy away from the path of the Red Monster and into a dark hole in the ground. They crouched low in the hole and the Red Monster shuddered and beat the ground beside them. Small lumps of earth came loose and rolled into the hole. Then it was over. The Other Harvest Mouse looked at Jeremy.

"You live on the other side of the field, don't you?" he said. "I'll take you home. Follow me."

And they jumped and scurried across the field until they reached Jeremy's nest. There they found Jeremy's mother shaking with worry.

"Oh, Jeremy," she cried. "You're safe. We didn't know where you were. We thought the Harvester wasn't coming until tomorrow. What an awful thing to happen."

"What's a Harvester?" asked Jeremy.

"Why," said his mother, "that Great Red Thing. It comes every year and takes away the wheat."

"But then we shan't have anything to eat," said Jeremy, who loved food.

"You wait and see," said his mother.

And the next day the Harvest Mouse family went off to look at a large and comfortable haystack.

"There," said Jeremy's mother. "That's where we're going to live all through the winter. Do you like it?"

Jeremy nodded. It looked so warm and inviting. He couldn't wait to move into the new haystack.

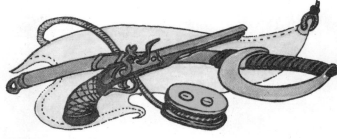

# The Pirate

Rachel and James lived long ago, in a little house by the sea.

In those days there were pirates on the high seas. So when Rachel and James played on the sea in their little boat, they pretended they were pirates.

When they played on land, they pretended they were soldiers in bright red coats. They dashed along the seashore, chasing and capturing hundreds of pirates.

One night there was a terrible storm. It blew so hard, their little house shook and shivered. But, next morning, the wind was gone and the sun was shining.

Rachel and James went down to the beach and found the wreck of a ship. It was very badly broken and would never sail again. Rachel and James explored it. They pretended they were shipwrecked sailors.

And then they found a chest in the wreckage. It was made of wood and held together by bands of iron. It was painted blue and had a rounded top.

"It's a treasure chest!" said Rachel.

James picked up the chest. "It's light. There can't be anything inside."

Rachel was disappointed "Open it to make sure," she said.

But the chest was locked. They couldn't get it open. So they pretended it was a treasure chest, anyway. They took it to the cliffs and hid it in a cave.

Next morning they returned to the shore again. But a strange man was there. He was clambering all over the wreckage, and shouting angrily.

Rachel and James hid behind some rocks. They didn't like the look of the man. His clothes were all torn and stained with salt. He had a black patch on one eye, and a great cutlass in his belt.

"He's a pirate!" squeaked Rachel. They both crouched lower behind the rocks. They heard the pirate bellowing:

"Where's my treasure chest? Who stole it from the wreck of my ship?"

He ran up the beach and spotted Rachel and James. He roared and ran at them, waving his cutlass over his head!

"Run!" shouted James. He pulled Rachel from behind the rocks and they started up the cliff.

Oh, how they climbed, with the pirate scrambling close behind them.

He was at their heels when they reached the top. But he couldn't run quite as fast as Rachel and James. They raced away over the fields, with the pirate puffing behind.

"Let's go home," cried Rachel.

"No!" said James. "The pirate would break down the door and catch us. We must find the soldiers."

When they reached the road, they didn't have to run any more. They met a troop of soldiers riding along.

When they saw the frightened children and the horrible pirate with his cutlass, the soldiers moved swiftly. The pirate soon found himself being chased by ten men in bright red coats!

They caught the pirate and hauled him off to jail.

Rachel and James were very grateful to be rescued. They told the soldiers about the treasure chest.

"We would give you half the treasure,"

James said, "but I'm afraid the chest is empty. There's nothing in it."

But the soldiers wanted to see the chest for themselves, so Rachel and James took them to the cave where it was hidden. The soldiers soon broke open the chest.

It wasn't empty after all. In it were a small bag of gold coins and a treasure map! The map was of an island in the South Seas, with a cross to show where the real treasure was buried!

"That map's no good to us," grumbled the soldiers. "We're not sailors. You won't catch us sailing off to look for treasure that might never be found!"

So Rachel and James gave the bag of gold to the soldiers, and kept the treasure map for themselves.

They kept it safe till they were grown up. Then they sailed far away over the sea to find the pirate's treasure.

# Eric's Breakfast

In the mountains of a very cold and snowy country there lived a forester called Eric. He was seven feet tall and had a small yellow beard.

Eric was in charge of all the fir trees which grew on the side of his mountain. He lived alone and high up, in a long wooden house. From his window he could see over the tops of the fir trees and down to the village in the valley below.

Eric was a slow-moving man, a very thoughtful man. Often he spent six weeks without talking to anyone. Not because he was unfriendly, but because he lived away from other people on his mountain.

One day in winter, Eric woke up early. It was six o'clock by his alarm clock. In the night it had started to snow. Already the new snow lay one foot thick on the ground outside.

Eric washed and dressed and lit his log fire. When the logs glowed red, Eric left the fire and went into his kitchen. He looked at his table and his cupboards.

"Errrrrr," said Eric in his slow, very careful way. "I think I will have eggs for my breakfast."

He opened the door of his pantry. But there were no eggs left. He had eaten the last six eggs only the day before.

"Errrrrr," said Eric. "No eggs."

Eric sat in his best armchair for a while and thought about what to do.

"Errrrrr," he said, after a few minutes, "I think I must go to the village shop and buy some more eggs."

The village shop was over five miles away, down at the foot of the valley. So Eric put on two more pullovers and a warm hat and gloves. Then he pulled on his great brown ski boots and clumped away to fetch his skis and ski poles.

The skis were long, and pointed at the front, and they shone with wax. Eric used them every day, and every day he cleaned off the old snow and put on a new coat of wax to make the skis run smoothly over the snow.

Eric strapped the long skis to his boots. He picked up his ski poles, and a knapsack to carry the eggs, and stepped outside.

It was snowing hard and Eric pulled down his hat until it almost covered his eyes. Then, using his poles to push himself along, Eric began his journey to the village shop.

Luckily the way was easier on the return journey. Half an hour later Eric skied into his front garden and took off his skis.

He went inside the house to the kitchen. He looked at his table and the shelves of his cupboards.

"Errrrrr," said Eric. "I think I will have bacon instead of eggs for my breakfast."

Soon he was sitting down to a large and tasty plateful of bacon. The fire glowed in the hearth. Eric was hungry and ate his bacon. Outside the snow had stopped falling at last.

"Errrrrr," said Eric. "If it doesn't snow tomorrow, I will go to the village to buy some eggs."

Then he sat in his best armchair and went to sleep beside the fire.

At first Eric was able to move along at a good steady speed. But the snow went on falling. It piled up more and more thickly on the ground, and Eric found the going harder and harder.

Eric could not remember when it had last snowed so hard. He pushed forward slowly on his skis. But, instead of going downhill to the valley, he found himself going uphill on the new snow.

Up and up went Eric. Higher and higher. At last he came to a complete stop. In front of him was an enormous white wall of snow and ice.

Eric looked over the snow toward the valley. It seemed further away than ever. He looked back the way he had come. There, in the distance, was his wooden house. A thin trail of wood smoke rose from the chimney. Eric suddenly felt rather cold. He thought hard for a few minutes.

"Errrrrr," he said at last. "I think I will not have eggs for my breakfast."

Eric made up his mind to go home.

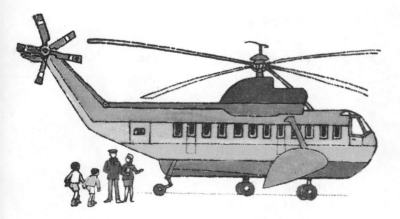

# Helicopter Rescue!

John and Francis were very excited. They had never flown anywhere before, and now they were going to have their first flight – and by helicopter too!

They had traveled overnight from London to Penzance with Father and Mother. This morning they were going to fly to the Scilly Islands. The Scillies are off the far southwest of England, and the weather is usually very warm. Even the sea there is quite warm.

The heliport – as helicopter airfields are called – was a small one. Not like London Airport where the two brothers had once gone to see the great airliners that traveled to every country in the world. Still, this time they were going to fly themselves, not just watch.

A helicopter doesn't have wings like ordinary airplanes, but a big rotor – like the blades of an electric fan – on top, which lifts it into the sky. It can fly forward, backward, straight up or straight down. It can even stay completely still, in the same place, in the sky.

John and Francis sat together by one window, and Mother and Father sat behind them, by another. When all the passengers were safely strapped into their seats, and the pilot had made sure that everything was working properly, the helicopter's engines began to roar and they bounced straight up into the sky.

Soon the people, cars and buildings on the ground looked like toys, and the land just like a map. Then they were flying over the sea.

Far below them, John and Francis could see a fishing boat. "Look," Francis shouted suddenly, "that boat's on fire!"

The pilot had seen it too, and flew the helicopter down for a closer look. Soon his voice came over the loudspeaker: "Attention everybody. As you can see, a boat is in trouble below. We have sent a radio message to the nearest lifeboat station, but we are going to stay and keep watch ourselves."

The fishing boat's engine was on fire, and although the four fishermen on board were doing their best to put it out, the fire was getting worse.

John called to the stewardess. "We must do something to help those fishermen," he said. "Couldn't we send a rope down to them?"

"There's nothing we can do," said the stewardess. "We don't have a rope."

"I've got lots of fishing line," said John, "and so has my brother Francis. If we tied it all together I'm sure it would reach the fishing boat. The fishermen could tie a rope on to the line. Then we could pull up the rope, and they could climb up it!"

The stewardess told the pilot and he said, "We'll try it."

So the co-pilot (all planes and helicopters have two pilots) joined all the fishing line together, tying a heavy bag to one end so that it wouldn't be blown by the wind. The pilot brought the helicopter even lower over the sea – so low that the wind from the rotor flattened the tops of the waves. Then, when everything was ready, the stewardess opened the helicopter door and the line was lowered.

Quickly the fishermen tied a thick rope to the line. The second pilot then hauled it up to the helicopter.

The fishermen took off their heavy rubber boots so they could grip the rope better. Then, one by one, they climbed up the rope. They were safe!

As the last one scrambled inside, the stewardess shut the door and the helicopter sped away.

Not a moment too soon! For just then the fishing boat exploded with a great roar, showering pieces of burning wood high into the air.

After that the rest of the flight seemed unexciting. And even though they had a marvelous vacation, the part John and Francis always remembered best was the rescue of the fishermen.

# The Lost Ring

The King was in a very bad mood. His favorite gold ring was nowhere to be found.

"Where's my gold ring?" shouted the King to his ministers in a terrible voice. Along the walls the great royal shields shivered and clattered at the sound of the King's voice. One by one they fell to the ground.

"Where's my favorite gold ring?" yelled the King again. BLOINNNGKLANG! went another royal shield.

"It appears to be still missing, Sire," replied the King's Chief Minister.

"Then find it, idiot," bawled the King. "Send my fastest warriors to every corner of the land. You will find the ring or lose your head!"

BLANGKLANGABERLOINNNG! The last three shields fell off the wall and the Chief Minister hurried away.

Unfortunately, because of the noise of the shields, he thought the King had said "Send my daftest warriors," not "my fastest warriors." He rushed into the courtyard and called for Elfric and Belfric.

"You're disgracefully daft," said the Chief Minister to Elfric and Belfric. "But go! Search the land. You must find the ring or we'll all lose our heads."

They made a plan. Elfric would search the eastern half of the kingdom, and Belfric the western half. Their horses were saddled. Soon the castle gates opened; Elfric turned

to the left, Belfric to the right, and off they rode beside the castle walls.

Being daft, Elfric and Belfric simply followed the castle walls, instead of turning away to east and west. Then, as they were both exactly halfway around the castle, they met, head on, with a tremendous bang.

Elfric was thrown high in the air. His trousers caught on a newly painted lance which someone had pushed out of a castle window to dry. And there he hung, legs and arms dangling, twenty feet above the moat.

Far below him was Belfric. Poor Belfric had been flung straight into the moat. His face was covered with weeds.

"I'll have their heads!" yelled the King, who had seen it all.

At that moment Elfric noticed something.

"Belfric," he called to his friend in the water. "Look. Down beside you. There's something shining at the bottom of the moat. Can you dive down and fetch it?"

Belfric nodded and disappeared beneath the surface. At last he swam to the bank. In his hand was a not-very-shiny object. He held it up for the others to see.

The King's Chief Minister gave a groan. Whatever it was, it was certainly not a gold ring. It looked more like an old chainmail sock.

"What!" roared the King. "I'll definitely have their heads!"

But the King's Chief Minister had been thinking.

"Sire," he said to the King, "that sock which Belfric has found. I see it bears the Royal Coat of Arms. Could it be one of yours?"

"What if it is?" said the King crossly. "It's Wednesday. I always change my socks on Wednesday."

"With your permission, Sire," said the Chief Minister. He took the chainmail sock by the heel and tipped it upside-down. A small gold ring fell out and landed with an expensive clink on the ground. The King blinked hard.

"My ring!" he shouted. "My favorite gold ring! But what was it doing in the moat?"

"Well, Sire," said the Chief Minister. "I expect it rolled off your bedside table and into the sock while you were sleeping. Then, when you changed your socks this morning, you threw the old ones out of the bedchamber window. And Elfric spotted the sock shining in the water."

The King was overjoyed. "Medals and chocolate biscuits all around," he cried. "Let's have a party!"

# Gidney the Goat

Gidney was a goat. He lived on a long chain in the garden at the back of a house in Ireland, and he ate everything that he could reach. He was beginning to have a bad reputation in the neighborhood because in the course of the past week he had eaten three socks and a pair of pajamas that were hanging on the clothesline of the next-door neighbors on one side, and six tennis balls and an expensive rug that were lying on the lawn of the neighbors on the other side. In addition, he was forever breaking loose from his chain and devouring anything that he could reach through the kitchen window that looked out over the back garden. This meant that Gidney's disgraceful stomach now held the remains of two cabbages, half-a-pound of bacon, three dishcloths and a large can of baked beans. It simply would not do, and Mrs. Flanagan, Gidney's owner, decided that she had better do something about it before all the neighbors came around and demanded to know what had happened to their socks and their tennis balls.

Unfortunately, before Mrs. Flanagan could decide what to do, there was an ominous click of the garden gate, and there was large Mr. Murphy from next door striding up the path in his best pin-striped suit. Mrs. Flanagan saw to her consternation that he was wearing only one sock. "Oh dear," thought Mrs. Flanagan, "here's trouble."

Bang, bang, bang, went Mr. Murphy with his big red knuckles on the kitchen window. "A word with you, if you please, Mrs. Flanagan!" he shouted.

Mrs. Flanagan opened the window.

"Good day to you, Mr. Murphy," she purred in her sweetest voice, "and what can I do for you this lovely morning?"

"You can find me something to keep my feet warm with," said Mr. Murphy, bending over the window-sill to stare angrily at Mrs. Flanagan, "because that thieving goat of yours has eaten all but one of my socks, not to mention my best pajamas."

Just then there was an awful tearing noise immediately outside the window, and Mrs. Flanagan saw Mr. Murphy's face swelling with rage.

"What the . . . !" he shouted, turning around to see what had happened. Too late. A large piece of pin-striped flannel trouser was disappearing into Gidney's mouth.

Mr. Murphy was so angry he didn't know what to say. He started to do a little dance of rage, hopping about clutching the place where Gidney had eaten a hole in his trousers, and making furious spluttering sounds.

"I'll teach that goat a lesson once and for all," he shouted, shaking his fist at Mrs. Flanagan. "Just you wait – "

BOINNG! went the elastic on Mr. Murphy's

suspenders as they flew from his trousers. Gidney was standing there chewing them as if they were the most delicious spaghetti.

"I'll get even!" bawled Mr. Murphy as he ran howling from the garden, clutching for dear life onto what was left of his trousers.

"Now, Gidney," said Mrs. Flanagan, wagging her finger sternly, "that was a dreadful thing to do. I shall have to be very severe with you."

Gidney just went on chewing in a very serene sort of way.

A moment later the garden gate clicked again, and there was Mrs. Flanagan's other neighbor, tall and spindly Mr. Furphy, coming up the path holding his tennis racquet.

"Mrs. Flanagan," he droned in his reedy voice, "I seem to have lost an expensive rug and six brand-new tennis balls, and I have reason to believe that your horrible goat has consumed them. I have therefore decided to call the police."

PLINK PLONK PLUNK! went Mr. Furphy's racquet. Gidney had plunged his teeth into the string and taken a healthy mouthful, which he was now cheerfully munching.

"I'll get even!" wailed Mr. Furphy as he leaped over the fence and back into his own garden.

Mrs. Flanagan was very worried. What could she do to stop Mr. Murphy and Mr. Furphy taking a terrible revenge on her and Gidney?

"I wonder what they like more than anything," she said to herself. "I know. Music. I will serenade them with my accordion."

She ran upstairs to the attic and brought the accordion down to the kitchen. Then she went to look for a cloth to dust it with. When she came back the accordion had disappeared and there was a strange noise coming from the garden. WHEEZ, SQUEAK, WHEEZ! it went. She looked out of the window, and there was Gidney with his head cocked to one side, listening with interest to the noises that were coming out of his stomach. WHEEZ! went the accordion as he breathed in. SQUEAK! it went as he breathed out. Soon he was playing a tune, and there, coming up the path together and dancing a jig, were Mr. Murphy and Mr. Furphy.

"Hee hee," they laughed, "that will teach him to eat everything in sight. Now we shall have music all day and Gidney will be too full of accordion to eat anything that belongs to us."

"I wouldn't be too sure about that," said Mrs. Flanagan, but she joined in the dance all the same, and so did Gidney who had decided that he quite enjoyed being a musician, even if it was rather filling.

# William Bear's Unusual Day

One morning William Bear climbed out of bed at his usual time. Large snowflakes fell past his window. The garden was already covered with snow.

"I'll put on my heavy winter suit," said William Bear.

He went downstairs to breakfast. A note on the kitchen door said: "Sorry. No Milk. Cows On Holiday. Yours, Milkman."

William Bear stepped outside his house. The sun shone brightly. There was no snow to be seen.

"I wish I weren't wearing my heavy suit," he said. "It's much too warm."

He went to the garage to fetch his car to drive to the railroad station. He opened the garage door and his car backed out without him.

"Wait!" shouted William Bear. But the car rolled away down the drive and turned onto the road.

William Bear ran after his car, but he couldn't catch it. As he ran, eight buses went past in a line.

He waited at the next bus stop. "I might catch my car if I chase it on a bus," thought William. But no buses came.

He walked to the railroad station to catch his usual train to the office.

"Sorry, Mr. Bear," said the Porter. "All the trains are going the other way today."

"Why?" asked William Bear.

"I don't know, really," said the Porter. "Suits me, though. I only have to stand on the one platform."

William Bear walked to the park. The sun was still shining but there was ice on the lake. All the ducks were running about on the ice.

William Bear ran to the lake to have a slide on the ice. But there was no ice and he fell straight into the water.

He sat on a bench to dry himself in the sun and two ducks skated past on the lake.

"I think I'll go home," said William Bear. "Today doesn't agree with me."

He turned into his street and walked toward his house. Mrs. Ostrich was in her front garden.

"Hello, Mr. Bear," said Mrs. Ostrich.

"Good morning," said William Bear.

"No work today?" asked Mrs. Ostrich. She looked at him in a rather strange way.

"No," said William.

"Oh," said Mrs. Ostrich. "*Really*?"

"Silly old featherbrain," said William to himself. But he must have said it aloud because Mrs. Ostrich gave a sudden scream.

"Henry!" she shouted to her husband. "Help! Mr. Bear has just been very rude to me."

Henry Ostrich arrived in his shirt sleeves. He was holding a large, rather soft tomato. He threw the soft tomato at William Bear.

William saw the tomato coming towards him. He jumped over the tomato and it went on by. Then William noticed that the tomato had turned around and was coming back. He ran to his house and the tomato chased after him.

William dashed inside his house and closed the door. But the tomato came straight through the door and followed William down the hall.

William ran up the stairs. The tomato followed. Faster and faster went William but he could not reach the top of the stairs. Each time he went up a step he seemed no nearer the top.

William's legs were very tired. Everything felt heavy. He kept on running, as fast as he could. One, two. As fast as he could. Three, four. As fast as he could. Five . . .

"William Bear," said a voice. William looked up. And there stood a tall bear with a big mustache. The tall bear looked like William's Uncle George. He was smiling.

"It's time to be back in your bed, William," said the tall man. "You've been in Dreamland. Goodbye now, William."

William blinked and looked around. Sure enough, there he was, in his own bed, in his own bedroom. It was morning.

"Was I really in Dreamland?" said William Bear to himself as he climbed out of bed. "It was a funny sort of place, whatever it's called."

Then he remembered. "Oh, yes. It's Uncle George's birthday tomorrow. I must buy him a nice present."

# Old Mrs. Jagger

Old Mrs. Jagger sat watching the rain. It fell steadily through the trees in her garden, it ran down her windowpanes, it dripped down her chimney. Old Mrs. Jagger was surrounded by the rain.

Hour after hour the rain fell. At first it ran off into the drains and disappeared underground. But soon the drains were full and the rainwater began to settle on the ground.

Then, because there was nowhere else for it to go, the rainwater crept under Old Mrs. Jagger's door and ran into her living room.

"It's a flood," cried Old Mrs. Jagger. "I'm being flooded!"

She rushed about with her mop and sponge, mopping and sponging up the floodwater. But the water was too quick for her and began to rise up her walls. One foot . . . two feet . . . three feet of floodwater covered the floor of Old Mrs. Jagger's house.

Old Mrs. Jagger jumped on her table. But the floodwater came up to her knees. She lifted a chair on to the table and stood on the chair. She was just high enough to keep her feet dry. But the floodwater was still rising.

"Oh dear," said Old Mrs. Jagger, "I'm too old for swimming. Whatever shall I do?"

Just then she heard a noise outside. It was the Village Fireman in his rowboat. The Fireman rowed up to the window and looked inside. He saw Old Mrs. Jagger standing on her chair which was standing on her table.

"Ahoy there, Mrs. Jagger," called the Fireman. "I'll soon have you out of there."

And he went to open the window. But the floodwater was too high and the window would not open.

"Ahoy there, Mrs. Jagger," called the Fireman. "I'll just try the front door."

And he rowed his boat to the front door. But the floodwater was too high and the door was stuck and would not open.

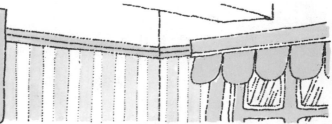

Old Mrs. Jagger saw a little wooden seat and a paddle.

The Fireman gave the rubber dinghy a push with his fireman's pole and it began to float slowly toward Old Mrs. Jagger.

"Ahoy there, Mrs. Jagger," called the Fireman. "Jump in the dinghy, please. And then paddle yourself to the front door."

Old Mrs. Jagger did as the Fireman said. The rubber dinghy wobbled a bit as she climbed into it. She dipped the paddle into the floodwater and the dinghy went backward. The she figured out what to do and pushed herself across to the window above the front door.

The Fireman was waiting for her. First he helped Old Mrs. Jagger into his rowboat. Then he reached inside the house with the fireman's pole and pulled out the rubber dinghy. He tied the dinghy to the rowboat and they rowed away to safety. The orange rubber dinghy bobbed along behind them.

"Nasty weather we're having," said the Fireman, as if nothing had happened.

"Yes," said Old Mrs. Jagger. "Thank you for saving me."

"That's all right, Mrs. Jagger," said the Fireman. "All in a day's work, you know."

Then Old Mrs. Jagger heard the sound of the Fireman's oars as he rowed away. SPLOSH TUG, SPLOSH TUG, splosh tug, splosh tug. And he was gone.

But the floodwater went on rising. Soon it was up to Old Mrs. Jagger's shoes.

Then she heard the Fireman coming back, splosh tug, splosh tug, SPLOSH TUG, SPLOSH TUG, went the oars. BUMP! went the Fireman's boat against Old Mrs. Jagger's front door.

"Ahoy there, Mrs. Jagger," called the Fireman. "I'll soon have you out of there."

Then Old Mrs. Jagger heard a strange noise. It sounded as if the Fireman was blowing up a tire or something. There was a lot of huffing and blowing from outside. HUFF WHOOSH, HUFF WHOOSH, HUFF WHOOSH.

Then the small window above Old Mrs. Jagger's front door opened and something round and orange-colored began to enter the house. It had round rubber walls like a balloon. It landed with a "plop" on the floodwater inside the house.

It was a small rubber dinghy. Inside it

# Fat Percy and the Tuba

Fat Percy Rundle used to play the tuba like any other tuba player. Until the day the triangle player in the Kipper Necktie Works Band fell on him.

The triangle player was a short thin man called Stanley. One day a hard gust of wind blew into the bandstand. It lifted Stanley clean off his feet. As he fell, Stanley landed on top of Percy the tuba player.

Then, as Stanley bounced off Percy's stomach, Percy gave out the richest, deepest tuba noise anyone in the Band had ever heard.

"OOOM PAHHH!" went Percy.

"Excellent!" cried the Conductor of the Band. And so Percy and Stanley became a very special musical team. When the Band gave their next concert, Percy lay on the platform instead of playing his tuba. And Stanley learned to jump up and down on

Percy's tummy at just the right moments.

"PAAAH PA-PA-PA-PA-PAH PAH PA-PAAH," went the rest of the Band.

"OOOM PAH OOOM PAH," went Percy.

"TING," went Stanley, who still found time to play his triangle as well.

The Kipper Necktie Works Band grew famous. More and more people came to hear the wonderful round, rich tones of Percy.

One day Percy looked into the audience sitting round the bandstand. He noticed a man in a big black hat. The man was staring at Percy. Percy waved to the man and the man gave Percy a little smile.

The next day he was there again, still looking at Percy.

Then the Conductor raised his baton and the trumpets began. Soon it was Percy's turn to play. At just the right moment Stanley made his first leap. He landed fair and square on Percy's tummy.

"Oooof!" went Percy. He turned white.

The Band stopped playing. How strange. It had never happened before. The Conductor started the Band again and they had another try. Stanley jumped.

"Ooooof!" went Percy. "Get off, please, Stanley," he said. "I can't do it."

It was dreadful. Percy had lost his tuba sound! Poor Percy. He looked so pale. Everyone was very sad. Percy went home and sat in his chair and stared at the wall. Later he went to see his doctor.

"There's nothing wrong with the rest of you," said the Doctor. "But you must never try to be a tuba again, nor must you even play a tuba for at least a year. You've been overdoing it. You must rest."

Percy went home and sat in his chair again. He felt sadder than ever. Then there was a knock at the door.

It was the man in the black hat who had been staring at Percy during the concert.

"Good morning, Percy," said the man. "My name is Black. I make musical instruments. I think I can help you."

To Percy's surprise, Mr. Black brought a large box into the house.

"This is my latest instrument," said Mr. Black. "It's an Electric Tuba. Listen."

He plugged in the box. Then, with a twirl of his arm he pressed a switch.

"OOOM PAHHH," went the Electric Tuba. It made the fullest and most beautiful tuba sound that Percy had ever heard.

"I don't believe it," said Percy. "How does it work, Mr. Black?"

Then Mr. Black showed Percy how to make all the different notes, from long deep ones to sharp short ones.

"Now you must practice," said Mr. Black.

Percy worked for hours and hours, until he could play the Electric Tuba as well as he himself had played.

At the next concert of the Kipper Necktie Works Band everyone was delighted. Especially Stanley, who still played the triangle but missed his old friend Percy.

The Electric Tuba, with Percy at the controls, was just what they all needed. Soon people came from far and wide once more to marvel at the Band.

# The Laziest Animal in the World

Mr. Cuthbert Lamont was a man of great learning. He studied the ways of animals and wrote miles and miles of important papers about them which he read to other men of great learning on special afternoons.

The other men of great learning listened carefully to Mr. Lamont until the sound of his voice put them to sleep. They woke up when Mr. Lamont was finished. Everyone was then ready for the tea and cakes which followed. Mr. Lamont was thirsty and hungry from so much learned talking, and the others were hungry and thirsty after their learned sleep. Everyone enjoyed Mr. Lamont's special afternoons.

One afternoon Mr. Cuthbert Lamont arrived to read one of his important papers. The hall was crowded with men of great learning. Some of them were already asleep.

"Good afternoon, er gentlemen," said Mr. Cuthbert Lamont from the platform. "Today I am going to talk to you about the laziest animal in the world. This animal is so, er lazy it may be five hours before I am, er finished."

Mr. Cuthbert Lamont lifted a square box on to the table in front of him. He opened the lid and pulled out a strange animal. It had long brown and yellow hair, a round head with large round eyes, a short stumpy tail and three long claws on each of its four feet.

"Gentlemen," said Mr. Cuthbert Lamont. "May I present to you the Three-toed, er Sloth. Usually the Three-toed Sloth hangs upside-down by its toes for long periods of time while it, er wonders what to do next. I will therefore place it thus."

And Mr. Lamont applied the Sloth to the arm of his chair. The Sloth took hold with his claws and quietly hung there, not moving at all, not looking at the ceiling, not looking at Mr. Lamont nor at the learned audience.

In the warm hush of the afternoon the other men of great learning slipped peppermints into their mouths and settled down in their chairs. Mr. Lamont began to read his learned paper.

"The most striking feature of the Three-

toed Sloth, a member of the Family, er Bradypodidae," droned Mr. Lamont to his audience, "is its sluggish movement or complete, er inactivity."

Learned heads began to drop forward on to their waistcoats. One or two snores rumbled in the air. Zzzz-zzz.

Two hours later Mr. Lamont was still talking away. The Three-toed Sloth hung peacefully from the arm of the chair. The other men of great learning listened quietly through their ears and snored softly through their noses.

After three hours Mr. Lamont was still talking away. The other men of great learning also seemed happy enough. But the Three-toed Sloth was not so happy. He felt lonely and far from home. A large tear came into his eye. It ran down the side of his face and fell on to the platform.

After four hours Mr. Lamont was still talking away. In the hall everything was still. Then, slowly, the Three-toed Sloth began to move. He swung along the arm of

Mr. Lamont's chair and climbed, tail first, down the chair-leg to the platform.

No one noticed that the Three-toed Sloth was on the move. He crossed the main floor of the hall. Nearly an hour later he reached the open door and passed through it into the next room.

Soon Mr. Lamont came to the last line of the last page of his paper. And there he stopped. There was a pause, then the other men of great learning woke up and loudly clapped their hands.

After a while they moved out to the next room for tea and cakes. They, and Mr. Lamont, had quite forgotten about their special visitor, the Three-toed Sloth. But when they reached the tea cart there he was, hanging upside-down from the tea cart. There was a smile on the face of the Three-toed Sloth, and all the cream cakes were gone.

"My goodness," said Mr. Lamont to the Three-toed Sloth. "You may be lazy but you know a good cake when you see one."

Mr. Lamont and the other men of great learning all roared with laughter at the lazy animal who had eaten their cream cakes. And the Three-toed Sloth, now full of cake and not at all lonely, smiled politely back.

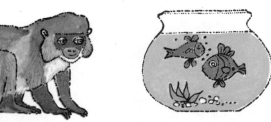

# The Pet Market

Aubrey and Barbara had never seen anything like it. In the United States where they lived, there were no outdoor markets at all, just very big stores. But this market filled a whole long street, with stalls – like big tables on wheels with roofs on top – all along both sides.

Aubrey and Barbara were on vacation in London with their mother and father. There are many street markets in London, but this one was a very special market indeed. Because it sold all different kinds of animals and pets. There were cages of puppies and kittens, and others of white mice and guinea pigs and hamsters. And there were all kinds of gaily-colored birds and fish.

"Let's buy something for Mommy and Daddy," Barbara said. "What about a little cat, or a puppy – they look so sad in those cages."

"Or a bird," replied Aubrey. "I think a bird would be better than a dog or cat."

But just then they saw an animal they both liked equally. It was a very strange little animal indeed, with a smooth head, pointed nose, broad flat back, and a small tail. And the oddest thing about it was that it wasn't covered with fur or feathers, but hard brown armor.

And it wasn't on a stall, or in a shop. In fact, it wasn't in any one place at all. It was racing down the street as fast as it could go!

"An armadillo!" shouted Aubrey. "An escaped armadillo!"

It seemed as if everybody in the market wanted to catch the armadillo. But the armadillo, whose name was Rivolino, didn't want to be caught – he was having far too good a time.

Soon, though, Rivolino's owner gave up. "I can't run any more," he gasped. "If you two can catch him you can keep him."

"Thank you," Aubrey and Barbara called over their shoulders as they raced on, up and down streets, through shops, around lamp-posts and in and out of the traffic. For no matter how fast Rivolino ran, or twisted, or dodged, he couldn't get away from the two children.

Finally, with a great effort, Aubrey overtook the little armadillo. Rivolino spun back the other way as fast as a spinning top. But there was Barbara!

Rivolino still knew one last trick. He stopped running, and completely rolled himself up into a ball.

Aubrey picked him up, very carefully. Slowly the little armadillo untucked his head and opened one eye. Then the other. He felt rather pleased with himself!

Later, Rivolino went back to America with Aubrey and Barbara and their parents. There he lived in a warm, sunny garden, with lots of insects to eat and nothing else to do but sleep and play chasing games with Aubrey and Barbara.

You see, armadillos can run quite fast, but they are even better at twisting and turning than they are at running. And Rivolino was the best twister and turner in the whole of South America, which is where he was born.

In and out between the stalls he raced with the crowd behind him. Everywhere he went people fell over themselves trying to grab him or dive on him. All the gaily-colored birds on the stalls stopped singing and flying, all the puppies and kittens stopped barking and meowing to watch the great chase. Even the fish stopped swimming to watch.

Aubrey and Barbara were soon leading the chase, along with the man who was Rivolino's owner and who kept shouting: "Rivolino, stop! Come back! Before you get run over! Stop!"

Soon they were out of the market. In the lead was Rivolino. Behind him came Aubrey and Barbara. Behind them came Rivolino's owner. And behind him came every one else.

# The Magician's Apprentice

One afternoon, long ago, an old man and a little boy arrived at a small town. They went to the biggest inn and asked to stay the night.

The innkeeper looked them up and down. The old man wore a funny pointed hat and a long black coat, both of which were old and nearly worn out.

"Have you got any money?" the innkeeper said.

"No, I'm afraid we haven't," replied the old man, "but I am Doctor Casals, the famous magician, and this is my apprentice Paul. I'm teaching him to be a magician too. If you let us stay here you will be richly rewarded, this I promise you."

"Look here," said the innkeeper, "I don't believe in magic, I only believe in money. So, since you haven't got any, go away!"

"Please, Doctor Casals," said Paul, "can't we magic some money to pay him?"

"Um, well no, Paul. You see, I'm not very good with money, the money I make always vanishes again very quickly."

Paul wasn't very surprised. Not many of the Doctor's spells ever came out right.

So the two of them tried their luck at another inn. And another. And another. But the same thing happened everywhere.

"I'll show them," he said. "So they don't believe in magic, eh? Well, for that I'll turn them all into – cabbages!"

Then the Doctor and Paul went off to a field where some cabbages were growing.

"Ah, there are some fine cabbages," the Doctor said. "Now for the spell."

"Please . . ." Paul tried to interrupt.

"Quiet!" shouted Doctor Casals. And began saying the spell.

The cabbage wriggled, then swayed. Finally it began to grow, and grow, and GROW.

"Something's wrong," said Doctor Casals. "The cabbage isn't supposed to grow."

"But I tried to tell you," said Paul. "It isn't a cabbage, it's a cauliflower."

The magician went pale. "Oh no," he said. "That spell only works for cabbages! I don't know what it will do to a cauliflower. What a terrible mistake! Why didn't I turn everybody into white mice? I could have done that as easily as anything. Now look what's happened!"

The cauliflower was now as high as a man. Then it was as high as a tree, and, when at last it stopped growing, it was higher than the church steeple and covered the whole town with its shadow.

But all the people of the town thought the Doctor had meant to make the cauliflower grow that big, and they all rushed to him to say how sorry they were for being unkind. They all begged him to stay with them – after getting rid of the giant cauliflower, of course!

The trouble was, Doctor Casals didn't know how to get rid of it. He tried every un-growing spell he knew. But the cauliflower didn't shrink an inch.

So Paul decided *he* had to do something. He began to climb up the cauliflower! Higher and higher.

At last, he reached the top. Far below him he could see the whole town, and all the townspeople looking up at him.

Then Paul said all the un-growing spells he had learned from the Doctor, and several other special spells which the magician used when things went wrong. The cauliflower gave a shake and a wriggle, and began to shrink and shrink until it was back to its usual size again.

Well, a lot of things were different in the town after that. The people were kinder to visitors, for one thing. And Doctor Casals and Paul lived there too. In fact they became partners and divided all the work of doing magic between them equally – except that the Doctor always left anything to do with vegetables entirely to Paul.

# The Horse Who Had Hiccups

George was undoubtedly the laziest and greediest horse in the stable. There was nothing he liked better than to spend his day just eating and sleeping; he couldn't bear to go hunting, and even trotting around a field he considered too much of an effort.

One morning, however, a very disagreeable thing happened. Mrs. Trumpington-Bumble, George's owner, came bursting into his stall, carrying a saddle and stirrups, and wearing her best hunting outfit. "Now wake up, George. You are going out hunting today," she said in her bossiest voice, throwing the saddle over George's back.

"Me? Hunting?" said George in an offended tone. "What about all those other horses? I don't want to go hunting."

"They've all got colds or rheumatism or something," said Mrs. Trumpington-Bumble, "so it has to be you."

"Well, I've had too much breakfast," said George. "I warn you, if you take me out, jumping all over those hedges and ditches and things, I shall get the most terrible hiccups."

"What dreadful nonsense you talk," snorted Mrs. Trumpington-Bumble. "Hiccups, my hat," and with that she jumped up on to George's back and he gave a most impolite groan at the weight of her.

"Come on," she said. "Gee up," and she kicked into George's round stomach and rode him through the gate and into the field. At the other end of the field was a huge hedge.

"I'm not going over that, if that's what you think," said George over his shoulder at Mrs. Trumpington-Bumble.

"Oh yes, you are," she shouted back. "We have got to hurry to catch up with the rest of the hunt."

Very well, thought George, she's asked for it, and with that he drew a deep breath and charged at full speed towards the hedge. Up they sailed, over the hedge, down the other side, and then across fields and more hedges and streams and ditches with George jumping higher and galloping faster than he had ever done before. Mrs. Trumpington-Bumble was feeling very pleased with him when quite suddenly he stopped – he could feel a rumbling inside his stomach.

"George! Whatever's the matter? Get a move on!" shouted Mrs. Trumpington-Bumble impatiently.

"Can't," said George. "I've got . . . HUWEERK!"

It was such a loud and violent hiccup that Mrs. Trumpington-Bumble was thrown off balance and fell into a bramble bush.

"I beg your pardon," said George, "but I – HUWEERK! – warned you, didn't I? HUWEERK!" he hiccupped again.

"I think you are pretending," said Mrs. Trumpington-Bumble, appearing out of the bush and climbing on to George's back. "I have never before heard of a horse having hiccups."

"Oh, really?" said George. "Well, I don't think I can stop having them unless I have several lumps of sugar and a large bag of oats – HUWEERK!" he went again, throwing Mrs. Trumpington-Bumble back into the bramble bush.

Eventually, after several more hiccups and several more falls into the bush, Mrs. Trumpington-Bumble realized that she would have to take George home. So she rode him very slowly back toward the house, and every so often George would

have a tremendous hiccup that threw Mrs. Trumpington-Bumble off into a puddle, or a mud patch, or a bush, which meant that by the time they were home Mrs. Trumpington-Bumble was covered with mud and brambles and bruises and quite unable to go hunting for several days, or certainly not before the other horses had recovered. This, of course, was exactly what George wanted, but he wasn't going to stop having hiccups until Mrs. Trumpington-Bumble brought him a great bucketful of sugar lumps and a big bag of oats.

"HUWEERK!" he went in the stable, extra loudly so that the walls shook.

"Pipe down, George," shouted the other horses. "Only a very lazy greedy horse would get hiccups out hunting."

"Quite true," said George, "but I am going to get a bucketful of sugar lumps and a huge bag of oats, which is more than you are. And," he added, "I shall never have to go hunting again with that big bossy lady."

# Albert Penguin's Birthday Party

It was Albert Penguin's birthday, and he was going to have a party. He had invited all his many relatives and a great number of his friends. There hadn't been such a party in Antarctica for a long time, and it was sure to be reported in the newspapers. Albert was very excited at the prospect. He washed his white shirt, dusted down his black jacket, rinsed his feet and his flippers, and prepared to receive his guests. Soon after four o'clock they started to arrive, the older ones waddling along at a dignified pace, the young penguins slithering across the ice on their tummies in their hurry to get at the delicious food.

And what a magnificent spread it was! On a huge table made out of blocks of ice there were shrimp cocktails and squid sandwiches and crisp plankton biscuits, and in the middle, covered with candles, was Albert's birthday cake. It was really an enormous fishcake coated with icing (made out of real ice and powdered snow) and Albert's mother had taken all morning to prepare it.

"Happy Birthday, Albert!" shouted the penguins, and they settled down to enjoy their tea. When all the sandwiches and biscuits had been eaten, it was time to cut the cake. Albert put on his funny paper hat and stood up proudly to blow out the candles.

"One, two, three," chorused all the guests.

Albert puffed out his chest. "Blow!"

"Whoosh!" went Albert as hard as he could at the candles. But none of them went out. All the penguins laughed.

"Come on, Albert, try again," they cried, clapping with their flippers. "Whooosh!" went Albert, even harder than before, but none of the candles went out.

"Weakling!" shouted the penguins in mocking tones, stamping their feet on the ice. "Lend him a pair of bellows!" squeaked one very sassy young bird.

"Whoooosh!" Albert blew for the third time, and nearly lost his balance into the cake. Still the candles burned. Albert mopped his brow; he was beginning to feel short of breath.

"I think someone else had better try," he said. "I don't seem to be very good at it," he added and he sat down to rest. Several other penguins approached the cake and prepared to blow together.

"One, two, three, whooooosh!" they went. The flames on the candles flickered in the

draft but still they did not go out. This was getting to be a nuisance, and besides, everyone was anxious to have a bite of the cake. Soon all the penguins were clustered around the table, blowing as hard as they could. The sound of their puffing was heard some distance away by a basking seal.

"I wonder what's going on," said the seal to himself. "Those penguins are behaving very strangely. I'll go and have a look," and he flumped along to the party.

"Having trouble?" inquired the seal.

"Oh, do come and help us," pleaded a very young penguin. "We can't blow the candles out on Albert's birthday cake, and they are beginning to melt the ice. If you don't blow them out, his birthday cake will disappear into the sea."

"Don't you worry," said the seal. "I'm an old hand at this sort of thing," and he drew himself up to his full height.

"Whooooosh!" he went. It was certainly a very hard blow and several of the smaller penguins were lifted off their feet by it,

but none of the candles went out.

"How very mysterious," said the seal. "These are certainly very difficult candles."

"Oh, what shall we do?" cried Albert's mother. "The table is starting to melt."

Just then an Arctic tern flew overhead. He was on his way from the North Pole to see his friends at the South Pole.

"Help!" shouted Albert, waving his flippers frantically. "Help us blow out the candles!"

"Sorry, old boy," croaked the tern. "I've flown a long way. Don't have much puff left." And he flapped on.

"I think I can solve your problem," said a deep voice, "so long as you give me a nibble of your cake."

Everyone turned around to see who had spoken. It was Whale, who was having a breather on the surface of the sea and had overheard what was happening.

"Watch your heads!" he shouted, and shot a great spout of water into the air. Up it went like a huge fountain, and down it came, *splash*, right on top of the birthday cake. Of course all the candles went out at once.

"Hooray!" shouted the penguins in delight. "Well done, Whale!"

"Hooray!" shouted Albert, cutting the cake, and handing it around. "What a wonderful birthday party."

Everyone had a delicious piece of cake, including Whale, who was given an extra large slice because he had been so clever in putting the candles out, and because he was after all slightly bigger than the rest of them.

# The Little River That Got Lost

One spring, high in the mountains, three rivers were talking.

"I flow to the blue sea," said the first. "Here in the hills I am small and fast and rocky, but when I reach the sea I am so wide that a man can hardly see across me."

"I too am small now," said the second river, "but when the sun has melted all the snow on the mountains I shall be big and deep and clean."

"Oh dear," thought the third river. For she was very small indeed, and unlike the others she stayed small no matter how much rain fell or snow melted. So she said:

"I'm just small . . . and very cold," she added. And she felt most unhappy.

"Hmm, well, as I was saying," went on the first and biggest river, "I'm extremely wide and long, and on my way to the sea I pass through many different countries and towns and cities; and lots of ships sail on me."

"I used to flow into the sea, too," said the second river, "but it seemed rather a waste. So now only a little of me reaches the sea; mostly I stay in a narrow valley with a big wall at one end called a dam. I am very important, because from there I water the fields which used to be too dry for anything to grow."

"Oh dear," said the third and smallest river, "I'm not really sure where I go or what I do – you see, I flow into another river, and then another. And those two join more rivers – I wonder where we all end up!" And she felt very sorry for herself.

In fact, there and then she decided that she would try to be an important river too. So when the snows started to melt, she made up her mind not to join up with other rivers, but to go all on her own. She was very excited, and raced off as fast as she could. She ran on for days and days, until she was completely lost.

"I know if I keep going downhill I ought to get to the sea," she said, but it became more and more difficult to *go* downhill, because the land got flatter and flatter, and she went more and more slowly. Then, in front of her, she saw hills covered with trees.

"Now what can I do?" she gasped. "I'm sure I'll never find a way through them; they look too high."

Well, she tried her best, wriggling in and out, dodging around the bottoms of hills and flowing through the valleys. But the hills kept getting higher, and she kept going more slowly, until finally, in a smooth space among the rocks, the little river . . . stopped!

The funny thing was, once it had happened it wasn't so bad after all. Because she made a very pretty pool.

Soon the birds and animals were telling each other about the lovely new place to wash and drink.

"Not deep and dangerous like some pools," they said, "not fast and powerful like the rivers, but gentle and still."

Soon all the small animals and birds began to go to the little pool, and soon, too, trees and flowers began to grow around her, and the children from the farms and villages came and sailed boats on her.

So the little river stopped worrying about how small she was, and forgot all about finding her way to the sea. She was happy to have become a beautiful little pool.

# Amanda and the Marmots

The Marmots live on a hillside in the mountains near St. Moritz. Marmots are small furry animals, and they have red-brown coats and mustaches. They make their homes in tunnels which they dig for themselves in the hillside.

In summer lots of people come to see the Marmots. Cars and buses full of people stop on the road near the Marmots' home, to see them play on the hillside.

Marmots are shy animals. They like people to come and see them. But if a stranger comes too near, the Chief Marmot gives a loud whistle, and all the Marmots dash back into their houses.

Sometimes, if the Chief Marmot says it is raining, the Marmots stay in their houses and do not come out at all.

The Chief Marmot is handsome and wise and has the biggest mustache of all the Marmots living on the hillside near St Moritz. The other Marmots admire their Chief's mustache and do what he tells them to do.

Amanda sat in the bus going to St. Moritz. She was very excited. Amanda had always wanted to see the Marmots and now the bus would soon be there.

But she wished the clouds would go away. There had been no sunshine at all that day. Then the sky grew darker and a few drops of rain began to fall.

They arrived at the hillside where the Marmots lived. Franco the driver stopped the bus. Everyone looked out of the windows. The hillside was empty. There was not a single Marmot.

"Oh dear," said Amanda to Franco, the driver of the bus. "I've come all this way to see the Marmots and they've gone. I suppose it's because of the rain."

Franco nodded. He felt sorry for Amanda. But he knew the Marmots well. They would not want to be out in the rain. All the same, Amanda looked very sad. Suddenly Franco opened the door of his bus.

"Come," he said, and took Amanda by the hand. "We will go and see the Chief Marmot."

They ran quickly up the hillside. Franco stopped beside a large rock and bent down on one knee. Amanda noticed a large hole in the ground next to the rock.

"Hey, Chief," called Franco. "It's me. Franco."

"What do you want, Franco?" said a voice from inside the hole. "It's raining."

Franco said, "I've got a little girl here called Amanda. She wants to see you."

"Not today, Franco," said the Chief Marmot. "Not when it's raining."

"Oh, come on, Chief," said Franco. "A little rain is nothing."

"You know how it is, Franco," replied the Chief Marmot. "If I come out for her, I have to come out for all the others. That way I can catch a cold."

Amanda was sadder than ever. She did so want to see the Marmots.

Then Franco said, "She's come to see your mustache."

"Yes," called Amanda into the hole. "Please, Mr. Marmot. I really want to see your mustache. I hear you have the most beautiful mustache of all the Marmots."

There was a sudden noise of running feet. A moment later the Chief Marmot appeared in the entrance to his house. His red-brown coat was bright and clean. His tail was smart and trim. And he wore the most magnificent bristly mustache.

"How do you do, Amanda," said the Chief Marmot smoothly. "I think it has just stopped raining."

And so it had. The clouds began to lift and a moment later the sun appeared. The Chief Marmot gave a loud whistle and soon the hillside was filled with jumping, dancing Marmots. Amanda played with them and had a most wonderful time.

"Thank you very much, Mr. Marmot," said Amanda to the Chief Marmot when it was time to go back to the bus. "I have enjoyed meeting you all."

"It's O.K.," said the Chief Marmot. "I hope we shall see you again, Amanda."

And he stood on the hillside and stroked his magnificent mustache, as Amanda's bus drove away on the road to St. Moritz.

# The Little Girl Who Loved New Clothes

Bubu was a little girl who loved new clothes. She had golden hair, light brown eyes which were slightly slanted, a small nose, and a very pretty mouth. She was tall and strong and enjoyed eating and sleeping, climbing on furniture, running races, and digging in the garden. She also liked wearing her mother's and her father's shoes – though these were much, much too big for her.

But the thing Bubu enjoyed doing best of all was wearing new clothes.

Once a week Bubu's mother let her choose a present for herself. Often she chose a toy car, or a duck, or a ball. But one day, when they were out shopping, Bubu saw the nicest coat she had ever seen. It was in a big shop, and it was a raincoat: bright yellow and shiny.

Bubu wanted that coat so much!

"Mummy, Mummy," she said, "what a lovely coat."

"It is, it really is," her mother answered. "Do you want to try it on?"

Well, of course Bubu did, and the coat fit perfectly.

Now Bubu wanted the coat more than she had ever wanted anything before, and she thought: "If Mummy has enough money to buy it, she will."

But the trouble was that Bubu's mother didn't have enough money to buy it!

"What can we do?" she asked Father. "Bubu needs a raincoat and I would so much like to buy her a yellow one we saw today, but I can't afford it."

Father couldn't afford to buy Bubu the coat either, and so for several days the whole house was sad – Bubu because she didn't have her coat, and Mother and Father because they weren't able to buy it for her.

Then, late one Sunday afternoon, all three of them went out for a walk. It had just

Soon, the firemen arrived, wearing big helmets and high boots, and carrying axes in their belts. They quickly put the fire out.

When everything was safe, Bubu's mother and father took her to meet the fire chief and the owner of the shop.

"This is the little girl who saw the fire first," said the fire chief. "Lucky thing she did – we were able to catch it before it had time to get very bad."

"I was looking at the yellow raincoats," Bubu said, "and I could see red coming from somewhere, and smoke."

"Well, I think that deserves a present," said the man who owned the shop. "How about one of those yellow coats you seem to like so much?"

So Bubu got the lovely shiny coat after all. And in fact she got more, for Father bought her some shiny yellow boots to go with it, and Mother bought her a little yellow rain-hat.

In fact, Bubu had all the new clothes she could possibly want. For a while, anyway!

stopped raining and they were almost the only people on the long street of shops. Bubu ran to look in the window of the shop which sold the yellow coat. She pressed her nose to the window and stared in, hard. There were the yellow coats! A whole rack of them!

But that wasn't all she could see. Even though the sun was shining, there seemed to be a light coming from the back of the shop. Rather a funny kind of light, too – red and smoky.

Bubu was sure something was wrong in the shop, but she couldn't yet think what. She stared again, very hard indeed. And then she knew!

"Daddy, Daddy," she cried, "there's a fire in the shop!"

"She's right," said her father and mother both together, "there is."

All three of them ran up the street until they found a telephone booth. Father called the Fire Department, and then they hurried back to the shop to watch what happened.

"They frighten me," said one deer.

"They eat strange things," said another.

"They are very untidy," said a third.

But Vicky disagreed. For of all the deer, she was the one who was the friendliest to their visitors. She would run up to people and sniff at them and their picnic lunches and eat from their hands.

And she was especially fond of one particular family. They came to the park three or four times a year. At first they came to see the house and the park. But, as they got used to Vicky running up to them and sniffing them and eating very gently from their hands, they came as much to see her as anything else. There were four people in the family: Mother and Father, and Robin and Jane, the two children.

Then one autumn afternoon, as Vicky was trotting through the trees with some of the other deer, they heard a little child crying. Vicky recognized the voice right away: it was Robin.

"That's the little boy I told you about," she said. "He must be lost. Let's go and find him."

But though the other deer were sorry for Robin, they didn't want to help him. "It's no business of ours," said one.

"His father and mother will find him, so why should we bother?" said another.

"They wouldn't help you if you were lost, Vicky," said a third.

All this made Vicky very angry. "I don't understand you," she said. "Little Robin is lost, and I *can* help, so I will."

Then she raced off as fast as she could

# Vicky and the Little Lost Boy

Vicky was a little deer who lived in a large park around a beautiful old house in the country. There were lots of bushes and flowers, and tall old trees.

Many people visited the house in summer. But the deer had different ideas on how to treat these strangers.

to find Robin. Well, like all deer, Vicky could hear things and smell things very well. So she very quickly found the little lost boy.

He was sitting under a tree crying and wishing he had not run off by himself into the trees. But the moment he saw Vicky he felt a bit better, and he stroked her head and ears and began to smile.

Just then Vicky heard Robin's mother and father and sister calling him in the distance. So, giving the little boy's hand a last lick to try to tell him not to worry, she ran off to find them.

Robin's father and mother and his sister were a long way away, and going in completely the wrong direction.

They were very pleased to see Vicky, but of course didn't know that she could lead them to Robin.

Vicky tried very hard to tell them – she ran around and around them, then ran away a little and came back. But they still didn't understand.

And they were still walking further and further away from where Robin was.

Then Vicky had an idea. She took Father's hand in her mouth and pulled him as hard as she could toward where Robin was. Then she did it again. She didn't hurt him because deer have no teeth in the front of their mouths.

At last they understood!

"She wants us to follow her," Robin's father said.

"She must know where he is," said Mother.

So off Vicky went, dodging through the trees with Robin's father and mother and sister, Jane, close behind.

She soon found Robin again, and the whole family gathered around to stroke her and thank her.

After that, Robin and Jane and Father and Mother came to the park more often than ever. They spent the time playing with Vicky, and always brought her a big bag of her favorite things to eat – lettuce, apples and cheese.

Among the other deer, Vicky became very famous. But even so, nearly all her friends stayed as shy of people as ever.

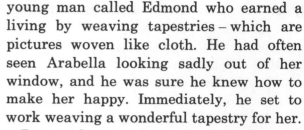

# Arabella and the Weaver

Once, many hundreds of years ago, there was a king named Otto who lived in a great white castle with golden turrets on a green hill surrounded by orchards of apple and cherry trees. King Otto would have been the happiest man in the world, but for one thing – his daughter Arabella.

For Arabella never laughed. Or smiled. Or even looked happy.

King Otto brought doctors from all over the world, but none of them could find out why she was unhappy. He proclaimed that any prince who could make Arabella smile could marry her and have half his kingdom. But though many handsome young princes tried, Arabella hardly even looked at them.

Finally, King Otto invited anyone in the land to come to his castle, and promised that whoever made Arabella laugh could claim any reward he wanted.

Now, in the town near the castle lived a young man called Edmond who earned a living by weaving tapestries – which are pictures woven like cloth. He had often seen Arabella looking sadly out of her window, and he was sure he knew how to make her happy. Immediately, he set to work weaving a wonderful tapestry for her.

But weeks went by, and while Edmond worked, hundreds of people flocked to the castle. Some told jokes. Some did tricks. Some sang songs. Yet Arabella only seemed to get sadder than ever.

At last, there was only one person in the kingdom who hadn't tried to cheer Arabella up – and that was Edmond. And, when his tapestry was finished, he too went to the castle.

King Otto looked at him very hard. "Well, what have we here?" he said. "What a miserable-looking specimen you are. Why, you are enough to make Arabella cry. Every one of my subjects has already tried. Tell me, why do you think you can succeed where all the others failed?"

"Because everyone else just wanted to win the reward," answered Edmond. "But I only want to make Arabella happy – that's all the reward I want!"

Well, the King led Edmond to Arabella, who was sitting sadly in her room. Her eyes were closed and she didn't even bother to look at them when they came in.

Edmond said: "I think it would be better if Arabella and I could be left alone."

"Not likely, my lad," stormed Otto. "I want to see what you are going to do!"

"Very well, Your Majesty," said Edmond. "The first thing I am going to do is this . . ." and he walked straight up to Arabella and kissed her!

Well, Arabella was so surprised that she opened her eyes. Wide.

Otto was speechless with anger, but Edmond just said: "Good, that's better. But that's just the first of my surprises. Here's the second."

And he took the furious King by his ear and pulled him out of the room.

Arabella had never seen anything so funny in her whole life. Slowly, she began to smile. Then to laugh. Finally, she laughed so hard the tears rolled down her cheeks.

And then Edmond unrolled the tapestry he had worked so hard to make.

Never had Arabella seen anything so beautiful. It had the sun, the moon, and the stars. It had trees and flowers, clouds and rainbows. And in the middle, it had Arabella – smiling happily – hand in hand with Edmond.

Then Edmond let King Otto back into the room. He was still furious, but when he saw how happy his daughter had become he completely forgot his rage. "Now then, young Edmond," he said, "you have done what nobody else could – you have made Arabella happy. You can have any reward you want."

"In that case," said Edmond, "providing Arabella agrees, I ask your permission to marry her. I won't need half your kingdom as well, Your Majesty, just her;!"

So they were married – the very next day. And from that time on, the white castle on the hill was full of laughter and joy. And beautiful tapestry pictures.

# The Sheep That Went to School

Johnny and Bill Dingle had a bicycle built for two. Every morning they rode to school together on it, and every afternoon they rode back home. One afternoon Johnny said to Billy: "I've got an idea. Let's play a trick on Miss Pout tomorrow."

Miss Pout was the teacher at their village school, and unfortunately she was very near-sighted.

"Let's take one of Farmer Drubble's sheep into the classroom and see if Miss Pout notices."

"Gosh, that's a good idea!" said Billy. "But how will we get the sheep into school?"

"I've thought about that," said Johnny. "We'll dress it up in Dad's old hat and raincoat, and balance it on the bicycle between us. Then we'll take it into the classroom before Miss Pout arrives, and sit it at one of the desks."

"Wow!" said Billy, clapping his hands in glee. It was a very exciting prospect.

And so the next morning a most extraordinary sight was to be seen on the road that led from Farmer Drubble's farm to the village school. There were Johnny and Billy pedaling their tandem bicycle, as usual, but in between them, balanced on the bar, was somebody else, dressed in a battered felt hat and an old raincoat. Or was it somebody else? The village people rubbed their eyes in wonder. A sheep in a hat and coat? No, it couldn't possibly be. Or could it?

When the boys reached the classroom with their new woolly school chum, the other children were very excited. Johnny told them to pretend not to know the sheep was there so that Miss Pout wouldn't notice it. Then they sat the sheep at a spare desk at the back of the classroom. It was still wearing the hat and raincoat. At nine o'clock sharp Miss Pout arrived with her bag full of books and pencils and rulers. All the children were sitting quietly at their desks, looking as if nothing unusual at all had happened.

"Good morning, boys and girls," said Miss Pout.

"Good morning, Miss Pout," they chorused.

"Baaa," went the sheep.

"Who made that silly noise?" said Miss Pout, peering around the classroom through her thick glasses.

"I'm sorry, Miss Pout, it was my chair creaking," said Johnny, untruthfully.

"Very well," said Miss Pout. "Now we will start with spelling. How do you spell 'House,' Billy?"

"Baaa," went the sheep.

Miss Pout swiveled around in rage. "Who is pretending to be a sheep?" she squeaked.

"Baaa," went the sheep.

Miss Pout could hear that the noise was coming from the back of the room. She strode between the desks till she was standing in front of the sheep.

"Young man, are you making those silly noises?" she demanded, wagging her finger angrily.

"Baaa," went the sheep.

Miss Pout peered closely at the figure in the seat, and then her eyes opened wide in horror. Just at that moment, there was a banging at the door and in strode huge Farmer Drubble.

"One of my sheep is missing, Miss Pout," he said, "and people in the village have told me they saw what might have been a sheep riding a bicycle to school this morning. Except it wasn't an ordinary bicycle," he added, "it was a bicycle built for two!"

"We didn't mean to steal the sheep, Farmer Drubble," said Johnny. "We only wanted to borrow it for the day."

"Yes, we wanted to teach it spelling," said Billy, trying to think of a good reason for taking the sheep.

"I know very well why you brought it here," said Miss Pout, "and I shall have to punish you, particularly as you have been untruthful. You will stay here after school today and do extra spelling."

"And then," said Farmer Drubble, "you will take my sheep back to the farm and help me clean out the pigsties. You have taken a sheep to work at school, now you can find out what work is like on the farm."

When Johnny and Billy got home that night they were very tired after all the extra work they had done at school and on the farm.

"What have you been doing to make you so sleepy?" asked their father.

"Oh, we took a sheep to school today," said Johnny, yawning.

"And it was very hard work," said Billy, closing his eyes, "because sheep can't spell."

Their parents looked at each other in astonishment. They didn't know what on earth the boys were talking about.

# The Pretty Shepherdess

Long ago a shepherdess named Ella lived on a mountain. She tended her flock of sheep and was very happy. When the sun shone she played follow-the-leader with her lambs, or strummed her guitar for the quiet old sheep. When it rained, she sat in her small house and sang songs while she spun and wove her wool.

On a summer day a proud young prince came riding past in his fine silk clothes. He saw pretty Ella playing with her lambs, and he fell in love with her at once.

He spoke to his servant. "Go and tell her to come here at once," he ordered.

The servant went to Ella and told her what the prince had said.

Ella laughed. "Tell the prince to come over here," she said, "for I must stay here and tend my sheep."

When he heard her reply, the prince was so angry, he rode away without a word.

He returned next day. Again he sent his servant to tell Ella to come. Again she laughed and refused. By then, the prince was *so* angry! He jumped from his horse. He marched to the river where Ella watched her sheep drinking.

"Who do you think you are, refusing to speak to me?" he shouted.

"I don't refuse to speak to you," she said. "Are you so lazy you can't walk a few feet to speak to me?"

The prince was most upset. Ella was the

first person who had ever spoken back to him, in his whole life! "But I love you," he cried. "I want to marry you! Come with me and live in my palace. You shall have servants to wait on you hand and foot. You shall never do a bit of work."

But Ella only laughed. "What, and be a great sissy like you?" she said.

Well! No one had ever called the prince a sissy. He *was* annoyed. He stomped up and down the river bank, glaring at Ella.

He stomped so hard, he knocked the edge of the bank into the river – and fell in with it himself!

"Help!" he cried. "I can't swim!"

Ella held out her long crook and he caught the end of the stick. Then she pulled him to shore.

He crawled from the water with his finery all soaked and muddy. Ella couldn't help laughing at the sight. He blushed, thinking what a sissy he really was, after all. Fancy falling in a river and being rescued by a girl! He muttered his thanks to Ella, and walked away, dripping. He didn't come back after that.

Ella was a bit sorry. It was rather nice to have a prince around, even if he was a sissy!

Many months later, the summer was over. It was time for Ella to leave the mountain, before the cold winter snows fell.

She started down the mountain, driving her sheep. But a storm blew up very fast. Soon Ella and all her sheep were lost and half buried in the drifting snow.

Poor Ella was afraid they would all perish on the spot, when a young shepherd came through the snow. He rounded up the sheep and led them down the mountain. He brought Ella to a little house, with a big stable beside it for the sheep.

He sat Ella before a warm fire to dry out. "I shan't laugh," he said, "even though you are wet, and not very pretty with mud all over your face!"

Ella knew that voice. She looked hard at the shepherd for the first time. He was really the prince! And it was his turn to come to the rescue!

"What happened to your fine horse and beautiful clothes? Why don't you live in your fine castle now?"

"I can have them whenever I wish," said the prince. "But all summer long I've been learning to be a shepherd, because I want to marry you, pretty shepherdess."

Ella laughed. "You're not a sissy any more," she said. "Now I'll marry you."

So Ella and the prince were married, and lived in his great palace. But when they grew tired of fine clothes and lazy living, they went back to the mountain and the sheep for a while.

And wherever they were, they were happy.

# Anthony Michael and the Fire

Anthony Michael sat in front of the fire. Outside the wind howled through the branches and blew great drifts of snow up against the walls of the house. It was getting dark, and the flickering flames of the fire were the only light in the room. Anthony Michael was all by himself because his mother was in the kitchen and his father was out in the forest chopping wood.

Crackle, hiss, flicker! went the fire. Anthony Michael loved to sit on the carpet in front of it and stare like a cat at the flames as they curled around the logs and licked at the pieces of coal. When he was by himself he liked to talk to the fire.

"Tell me a story, fire," he whispered.

"A story?" said the fire. "Well, let me think, what sort of story would you like?"

"One about knights in armor and fierce dragons and ladies locked up in a castle," said Anthony Michael eagerly.

"Oh, I'm not sure you are old enough for such tales," said the fire.

"Yes I am," said Anthony Michael indignantly. "I am eight years old and I have read lots of books."

"Do you know how old I am?" asked the fire. "I am older than anything you can possibly imagine, and I know more stories than you could possibly learn in your lifetime. You mentioned dragons just now – I used to live inside the mouths of dragons, you know."

"Yes, I did know," said Anthony Michael, "and you used to shoot out and burn the lances of the knights who came to kill the dragons."

"Yes, I am afraid I get excited rather easily," said the fire in a resigned sort of way. "Now if you want a story you had better stoke me up, because I'm needing a bit of spark, but remember to treat me carefully. I don't want to get into trouble . . ."

But it was too late. Anthony Michael was so excited at the prospect of a story that he bent down into the log basket, picked out several big logs and some large pieces of coal, and threw them on to the fire. Crack, sizzle, whoosh! went the fire, wrapping great big flames around the dry wood.

"Oh, oh," shouted the fire. "That's too much! I warned you! This wood is awfully tasty!"

And he started to roar and shoot huge flames up into the chimney. Sparks from the burning logs cracked and jumped into the air, and Anthony Michael could feel the heat reddening his cheeks.

"Oh please, fire!" he cried. "Don't burn so fast!"

"I can't help it," shouted the fire. "You will have to do something, or I shall burn the chimney down!"

And already lumps of smoldering soot were falling from the chimney. Anthony Michael was very frightened. Just as he was wondering what to do, he heard the sound of heavy boots being stamped in the hall, and then his father came bursting into the room.

"What have you been doing to the fire?" he asked in an angry voice. "There are sparks coming out of the top of the chimney. We shall have to call the fire department."

But just as he reached for the telephone, there was a loud rushing noise in the chimney, and a huge mound of snow came tumbling down on to the fire. An extra strong gust of wind had blown it off the chimney-top.

Ouch, splutter, psss! went the fire as the snow fell on it and the wet logs gave off a thick blue smoke. The big flames had all gone out: there was just a tiny blue one flickering feebly in a corner of the smoldering grate.

"I knew this would happen," said the fire in a small voice. "I said that you must treat me carefully, and now I am much too damp to tell you a story. You are just very lucky that the snow fell down the chimney, otherwise . . ." But before it could finish the sentence, the fire gave a small spluttering sneeze, and went out.

"You certainly are very lucky, my boy," said Anthony Michael's father as he tucked him into bed. "You see, the fire is good to us and keeps us warm so long as we watch it and never play games with it. Now, if you like, I will tell you a story."

"What about?" said Anthony Michael.

"Well, once upon a time there was a fierce fire-eating dragon . . ."

But Anthony Michael was already asleep.

# Paolo's Soccer Ball

Paolo was six years old and he lived on the edge of a big city by the sea in Brazil. More than anything else in the world, Paolo wanted to be a famous soccer player, but his parents were so poor that they couldn't even afford to buy him a ball to play with. Paolo's father was a fisherman, and the money he earned was only just enough to provide them with food and clothes.

"One day maybe I will have a big catch in my net," he would say to Paolo, "and then we will buy you a soccer ball."

So every morning Paolo stood at the window to watch his father coming back up the street from his night's fishing, hoping that his basket would be full of fish. His father would come through the door, put his basket on the table, and remove the cloth that covered the fish.

"No soccer ball today, Paolo," he would say, smiling sadly at the boy and pointing at the two or three fish that lay on the green leaves at the bottom of the basket. "Maybe tomorrow, huh? Yes, maybe tomorrow," his father would add, hoping it would be true.

Then Paolo would wander down to the long golden beach that curved around the bay. All the boys of the big city came down to the beach to play soccer, and Paolo would stand with his friends on the edge of a group, longing to be invited to join in the game. But they never were, because there were always too many players and not enough balls.

One sunny morning, however, everything changed. Paolo looked out of the window and there was his father coming up the street carrying a basket that was obviously much heavier than usual. He came through the door and placed the basket on the table. Then he pulled off the cloth and smiled the biggest smile that Paolo had ever seen. The basket was full to the top with gleaming silver fish. Paolo jumped up and down and clapped his hands in excitement.

"May I have a soccer ball, Father?" he asked.

"Of course you may have a soccer ball, Paolo. We will go at once to the market to sell the fish and then we will go to the shop that sells soccer balls.

One hour later Paolo was running down to the beach carrying a brand-new ball. It was white with black spots and had the names of Brazil's national soccer team on it. Paolo's friends clustered round him in excitement, and at once they marked the boundaries and made nets out of their shirts. Then they started to play with Paolo's new ball. It was wonderful. Paolo had never been so happy in his life.

Suddenly a dreadful thing happened. Paolo aimed to kick the ball toward the goal, but it spun off his foot and sailed out into the sea. Paolo and his friends rushed into the water, but the ball had been caught by a fast-flowing current and was bobbing away out of their reach. Soon it was way out over their heads and they had to give up the chase and just watch helplessly as it drifted away till it was no more than a tiny

white blob far out on the open sea. Poor Paolo was heartbroken. He sat down in the shallow water and cried and cried. He had only had his soccer ball for a few minutes and it might be months before his father could afford to buy him another one. When he went home and told his father and mother what had happened, they were very sad, too.

"But perhaps we shall be lucky," his father said. "Perhaps I shall have a big catch again tonight. It sometimes happens that way, you know."

Paolo didn't believe it. He went to bed feeling very miserable and he didn't even bother to look out of the window to see his father coming back in the morning. Then he heard his father calling him from downstairs.

"Come down, Paolo, I have something to show you." Paolo ran down the stairs.

"What is it, Father?" he said.

His father was standing over the basket on the table. It was still covered with the cloth.

"Paolo, I want to show you the most extraordinary fish that ever came out of the whole wide sea."

Then he pulled back the cloth, and there, lying among the crabs and shrimps and silver fish, was Paolo's soccer ball. What a miracle! His father had pulled it up in his fishing net.

"Now you know that if you want to be a famous soccer player, you have to learn to kick straight," said Paolo's father. But Paolo was already out of the door and running down to the beach with his favorite and most treasured possession.

# A Very Friendly Tail

Ronald the Setter was really a very nice dog, but he wagged his tail too much. Swish, swish, back and forth it went whenever he saw somebody he liked, and because he was very friendly and there were lots of people that he did like, it was going back and forth all the time. But it was such a long bushy tail that he was always causing trouble with it. Every time he wagged his tail, Ronald knocked things over; vases full of flowers would fall down and spill over the carpet, and cups and plates would be swept from the table. The trouble was, it was very difficult to get angry with him because everybody knew that he was only wagging his tail to be friendly.

One day, however, somebody did get really cross with Ronald. It was Mr. Clink, who owned the china shop at the corner of the street. Ronald had wandered into his shop on one of his morning walks and because he liked Mr. Clink very much, had wagged his tail extra hard. Crash, splinter, tinkle, went a whole shelf of Mr. Clink's precious china. Splinter, tinkle, crash, went another.

"Stop wagging that beastly tail of yours," shouted Mr. Clink, trying to push Ronald out the door. But Ronald thought Mr. Clink was patting him, so he wagged his tail even harder. Tinkle, crash, splinter, went a third shelf of china. Poor Mr. Clink. It really was a dreadful mess. There were broken pieces of cups and bowls and plates and saucers scattered all over the floor of

his shop. He sat down on a box and buried his head in his hands. Whatever would he do? Suddenly Mr. Clink had a brainstorm. He would make Ronald clear up the mess by tying a brush to his tail. He ran out to the back of the shop to fetch a brush and some string. Then he tied the brush to Ronald's tail. Ronald seemed a bit surprised at having a brush tied to his tail but he still continued

to wag it, and in no time at all he had swept all the broken china into the dustpan that Mr. Clink held ready to catch the pieces.

Then Mr. Clink had an even better idea. His shop needed painting, and what better way of painting it than to tie a paint brush to Ronald's tail and get him to wag it at the wall? He tied on the brush, dipped it into the paint bucket, gave Ronald a large bone to keep him happy and wagging, and stood him in front of the wall. It worked like

a charm. Splish, splash, went the brush on the wall as Ronald wagged his tail, and the wall started to change color. Every few minutes Mr. Clink would run over and dip Ronald's tail in the paint and move him along a bit with his bone to paint a different part of the wall.

Mr. Clink was just beginning to feel that this would make up for all the broken china when something quite unexpected happened. Out of the corner of his eye

Ronald had spotted a cat outside the window. In a flash he was out of the door and was chasing it madly up the crowded street. But the wet paint brush was still tied on to his tail. Splosh! it went against the policeman's legs as Ronald raced past, leaving a huge paint mark on his trousers. Slap! it went against the fat lady bending over to buy brussels sprouts in the market.

All along the street people were slapped and splashed by the wet white paint brush on Ronald's excitedly wagging tail as he chased the cat, and soon all the people were chasing him, too. Ronald ran into the park but the cat had climbed up a tree, so he just stood and barked cheerfully up at it. Then he turned round and saw the enormous crowd of people running toward him.

"How wonderful," he thought. "All these nice people have come to talk to me." And he gave his tail such an extra-friendly wag that the paint brush flew off the end and hit an old man who was asleep on a park bench. It didn't please the old man at all and he joined the large crowd that had gathered around Ronald. They were looking very fiercely at him.

"Now look here," said the policeman in a stern voice. "You've got to do something about that tail of yours. You have been doing a great deal of damage with it. If you're not careful I shall have to tie a bell on the end of it so that everyone will know you are coming."

But Ronald wasn't listening. He was having such a lovely time surrounded by so many people, even if they were angry, that he just went on wagging, and in a few minutes they had forgiven him for covering them with paint. After all, you can't really be cross for long with a dog who never stops wagging his tail.

# Hummmphrey the Spinning Top

Billy had a big tin spinning top named Hummmphrey. That was his proper name, but Billy called him Humph for short.

Humph was a handsome top. He was painted in bright stripes. On top, he had a shiny gold knob. When it was pumped up and down, Humph would spin around.

One day Billy took him to the park. "My friend Jasper is bringing his top to the park too," he told Humph. "We're going to have a contest, to see whose top can spin the longest. So you be a good top, and spin as hard as you can."

Humph was very excited. He'd never been in a contest before.

Jasper was waiting for them at the park. He had a big blue spinning top. "I call him Lark, because he sings like a bird," said Jasper.

Billy and Jasper chose a big clear space covered in cement. It was very smooth – just right for spinning tops. They balanced the tops on their points and pumped the handles. "Hummmm," went Humph, starting to spin. "Himm, himm, himm," went Lark, in a very musical voice.

Soon Humph was spinning faster than he'd ever spun before. He hummed joyously.

At last Billy let him go. Humph zoomed across the cement. He skimmed along at a wonderful speed. "Wheeeee," he cried.

Suddenly Billy shouted: "Look out! You're going to crash!"

In the excitement, Humph had forgotten all about Lark. Now he saw Lark spinning right beside him!

Humph tried to dodge out of the way, but it was too late. *Donk! Clang!* went the two tops as they struck. Lark wasn't hurt, but he lost his balance. He fell over on his side and rolled to a stop.

Humph wasn't hurt either. He didn't lose his balance, but he was knocked high in

the air. He landed on his point, still spinning as fast as ever!

Humph tried to steer back to Billy, but he was out of control! He headed straight for the hedge at the end of the park. He closed his eyes, expecting to hit the hedge. But he missed it! He zipped clear through a small gap at the bottom!

When he opened his eyes, he was in a garden! He swooped through a cabbage patch, unable to slow down. A frightened bird squawked and flew from his path.

"Who's that playing in my cabbages?" called Mrs. Mullins, coming from the house.

At that moment Humph reeled from the cabbages, on to the path. "Rumble, rumble," went his point on the flagstones. "Hum, hum," went his voice. It wasn't a happy hum any more, because Humph was scared. He didn't like being lost and out of control.

Mrs. Mullins was scared, too. She yelped and jumped behind a rose bush. "What is it?" she cried. "It looks like a tiny space ship, full of little green men from Mars!"

(Mrs. Mullins had a wonderful imagination, though, to be honest, Humph *did* look a bit like a flying saucer.)

Spinning almost as fast as ever, Humph whizzed up the path, past Mrs. Mullins. He bumped into the doorstep, bounced over it, and twirled into the kitchen!

"Oh, where am I now?" he wailed. He was so dizzy from all his spinning, he couldn't see straight. He felt himself slowing down. He wobbled into the hall.

A moment later Mr. Mullins, coming home for his tea, opened the front door. What a surprise he had when Humph popped out and rolled to a stop at his feet.

"Why, it's a top!" he said, picking up Humph. "Now, why would Mrs. Mullins ever be playing with a top?"

Just then along came Mrs. Mullins, who had got over her fright. She laughed when she saw Humph. "He gave me a scare," she said. "I suppose he came from the park. Let's see if we can find his owner."

Humph was glad to hear that. He was still a bit dizzy, and quite lost. They took him to the end of the garden. There, peeking over the hedge, was Billy. Mr. Mullins gave Humph to him.

Humph was happy to be back with Billy. He promised himself to be more careful in his next spinning contest!

# The Sun Lover

Cromwell lion lived on a wide African plain, where he could see for miles. He loved the sun. Every morning he watched it rise over the eastern edge of the world. Then he lay and basked in its warm light.

In the heat of the day, the other lions hid from the sun, in the shade of a tree. But Cromwell stayed where the sun could touch him, toasting happily.

Every evening, when the sun set behind the western hills, Cromwell was sad, and sighed for the morning light.

One evening George lion listened to Cromwell sighing as the sun set. George laughed. "What will you do if the sun never comes back?" he asked Cromwell.

What a terrible idea! "What do you mean?" gasped Cromwell, very frightened.

"Well, the sun goes to the western hills every night," said George. "It must like them. Some day it may decide to stay."

"No, no!" cried Cromwell. "The sun never stays still. It travels all night, hiding behind the hills. Otherwise, how could it rise in the east each morning?"

"Oh, I wouldn't know about that," said George. He never bothered to *think* about things. But he did like teasing other lions. So he went off to sleep, laughing because he had Cromwell worried.

Poor Cromwell lay and worried all night, too. He was so afraid that the sun wouldn't come back, he didn't sleep a wink.

But at last the sky turned from black to grey. And, from behind the eastern edge of the world, up shot the sun!

Cromwell ran to George and shouted happily: "Look! The sun's come back. You were wrong about it staying away!"

George was grumpy at being woken early. He growled at Cromwell: "I didn't say it *would* stay away. I said it *might!*"

But Cromwell was so happy to see the sun, he wasn't worried by what George said. Not till the middle of the day, that is. Then the sun began its long slide down the sky, toward the western hills.

"I wonder what's behind those hills? I wonder why the sun goes there every night?" he said.

He just *had* to know. He leaped up. "I'm going to see where the sun's going!" he cried, and ran off toward the west.

The other lions were worried, but George laughed. "I expect old Cromwell's just got a touch too much of the sun," he said. "He'll come back when he cools down."

Meanwhile, Cromwell raced across the plain on his strong lion legs. Zebras and giraffes fled from his path, but he barely noticed them. A herd of elephants trumpeted and stampeded, but he raced between their pounding feet without fear.

Cromwell lion hated getting wet, but that day he swam a great river without stopping to think about it. He hated the dark jungle, but he plunged straight into it.

And all the while the sun raced ahead.

At last Cromwell reached the top of the western hills. There, covering all before him,

lay the boundless sea. And at the farthest edge, was *the sun, falling into the sea!*

Cromwell was horrified. The sun's flames would be put out forever by the waves of the sea! He roared and bellowed at the sun, warning it of the danger. But the sun ignored him. It sank into the sea in a blaze of gold, and darkness fell.

Cromwell fell sobbing on the brink of the sea, and didn't stir again.

Not until morning, that is, when the sun rose in the east and smiled upon him.

Cromwell leaped up and roared good morning to the friendly sun, which was just as bright as ever. Then, thinking deeply, he returned, through jungle, river and elephant herd, to his lion home.

"I've decided what happens at night," he told George. "The earth must be a round ball, like the sun. We can't see the sun at night because it's busy shining on the other side of the earth. But every morning the sun comes around to our side of the earth."

"Silly Cromwell. I *said* you had a touch of the sun," teased George lion.

Which one do you think was the silly lion?

# Franz and the Huge Friendly Bird

Franz was very bored. He had gone to stay with his large gloomy Auntie who lived in the Black Forest, and she did nothing except sit in her rocking chair eating apple strudel all day long. Franz had no one to play with and no one to talk to because his Auntie didn't like talking, and anyway her mouth was always so full of strudel that she couldn't get any words out without covering the carpet with crumbs. It really was very dull, and Franz wished very much that he could go back home.

One day he was walking through the forest, feeling particularly glum, when there was a loud flapping sound above him. He looked up and there, perched on a branch just above his head, was a huge bird. It was green and yellow with an enormous beak that made it look as though it was grinning from ear to ear.

"Hello, Franz," said the bird in a cheerful voice.

"Hello," said Franz. "Who are you?"

"I am known as the Huge Friendly Bird," said the Huge Friendly Bird. "I live in this forest because it is very dark and gloomy, and because so many people come wandering through here alone when they are feeling miserable. It's my job to cheer them up."

"But how did you know I was miserable?" said Franz.

"Well, people pass me messages – other

birds, rabbits, squirrels – you know, the chatterbox types. We knew you were pretty bored with your Auntie. I must say I would be too, fond as I am of apple strudel."

The Huge Friendly Bird chuckled and licked his beak. Franz decided that he liked him very much.

"I want to go back home," he said. "I'm so tired of my gloomy strudel-eating Auntie, and it's another whole week before I'm supposed to leave. What shall I do?"

"Let me think," said the Huge Friendly Bird. "How old are you? Seven? Eight?"

"I'm seven," said Franz.

"Excellent," said the Huge Friendly Bird. "Then I'm sure you enjoy building things. You can come and help me build my new nest. Would you like to do that?"

"Yes, I'd love to," said Franz. So Franz followed the Huge Friendly Bird as he flapped ahead along the path to where he was building his new nest. When they arrived Franz saw that it was the most enormous nest he had ever seen in his life, even in picture books. It was just like a giant four-poster bed, except that it was made of twigs and leaves and grasses, and it was the same height off the ground as a bed, so Franz could easily climb up onto it. Mrs. Huge Friendly Bird was busy tidying it up when they arrived.

"How do you do, Franz," she called. "Come on up and have a nut or something."

Franz climbed up and marvelled at the size and strength of the nest. It didn't give under his weight at all.

"But your nest is built, Huge Friendly Bird," he said. "Why do you need me?"

"Ah, I want you to build me a sign to put outside the nest that will tell everyone that we want to cheer them up."

So Franz set to work; he began by chopping down branches, then sawed them into planks, and finally hammered them together to make a huge sign board.

"Wonderful," said the Huge Friendly Bird when Franz showed him what he had done. "Now you must write on it. I can't do it,

because my spelling isn't very good."

So Franz wrote in large letters of white paint: MR. AND MRS. HUGE FRIENDLY BIRD. OPEN TO MISERABLE VISITORS, and they stuck the sign board in the ground beside the nest.

"All we have to do now," said the Huge Friendly Bird, "is to get your sad Auntie to come along."

Franz thought that would be rather difficult, but when he told her about the Huge Friendly Birds and what he had done, she was so curious that she went along to see for herself. And Mr. and Mrs. Huge Friendly Bird were so nice and cheerful that after a few minutes she started to smile and talk, and think of exciting things for Franz to do with his holidays. So Franz really enjoyed the rest of his stay, because every day they would go to tea with the Huge Friendly Birds, and his Auntie wasn't gloomy any more and didn't eat nearly so much apple strudel. Franz decided that soon all the miserable people in the neighborhood would be visiting the Huge Friendly Birds, and that made him very happy.

# The Magic Emerald

There was once a King who had a magic emerald. He didn't know it was magic. But it was beautiful, so he had it set into a gold ring, and wore it all the time.

He wore it one day when he went on a picnic with the Queen and their princess daughters – Amaryllis, Angela and Alice.

Amaryllis was the biggest princess. She had a very royal manner. Everyone said what a *princessy* princess she was, and what a noble queen she would be when she was grown up.

Angela was the sweetest princess. Everyone said how sweet she was, and admired her big blue eyes and golden ringlets.

Alice was the smallest princess. She didn't look princessy like Amaryllis, or sugary like Angela. She looked just like a little girl. Everyone loved her best.

On the picnic, everyone did just what he wanted. The Queen found a nice grassy spot and set out the food. The King found another grassy spot and had a snooze. Princess Amaryllis sat on a tall rock, pretending it was her throne. Princess Angela made a chain of pretty flowers to wear in her hair. Princess Alice went wading at the edge of the river.

Suddenly Alice stepped on a slippery rock and fell into deep water. The river caught her and began to carry her away.

"Help! Help!" she called.

But no one could help her, for none of them could swim. The King, the Queen and the two princesses ran along the bank. They all screamed for help.

"Oh, I wish someone would save my darling Alice!" cried the King.

As always, the magic emerald made the King's wish come true. It couldn't jump in the river and rescue Alice itself. But it sent out a powerful magic call.

The call was heard by a wandering lad named Bruce, who was half a mile away from

the river. He never realized that he heard the call only inside his head and that his ears heard nothing at all.

Quick as a flash Bruce leaped over a hedge, ran across a field, hopped over a wall, charged through a wood, and dove into the river. He caught poor drowning Alice and swam to the bank with her.

Alice was saved. Everyone was so happy they all had to do something to thank Bruce. The Queen invited him to join their picnic. Princess Amaryllis called him a hero, in such a royal way that he felt like a knight in shining armor. Princess Angela set her flower chain on his head with her own fair hands. Princess Alice kissed his cheek and thanked him for saving her life. And the King gave him his beautiful emerald ring!

They had a merry picnic. But when it was over, Bruce stood up to say goodbye to everyone. He had nowhere special to go, for he was a real wandering boy, without a home. He didn't want to leave, for he already loved the whole family.

"I wish I could stay with them," he murmured to himself. No one heard him — except for the magic emerald. It set to work.

It woke the King, who was having his after-picnic snooze. "What's that? Leaving us?" he cried, waking up with a jump. "Oh, no no no! You come and stay with us."

"What a good idea!" said the Queen. "There's plenty of room at the palace."

"Yes, yes," shouted all three princesses. "You must come home with us, and stay as long as you please."

So Bruce went with them. And because he always wished it so, he never left them. The magic emerald made sure of that.

When he was grown up, Bruce married Princess Alice, and they had three little princesses of their own.

But in all his long and happy life, Bruce never knew his emerald was a magic stone. When he was an old man, he gave it to his eldest daughter. And when she was old, she gave it to *her* eldest child.

So, for many, many years, the magic emerald has passed from parent to child. None has ever known of its magic. But all have lived happy lives, with every wish coming true.

# Abel's Dream

Abel lay in bed and listened to the rain falling on the roof. The roof was made of tin, so the sound of the rain falling on it was like a drum beating very fast, or like horses' hooves thundering over the ground. And as he fell asleep, he dreamed that he was riding one of the horses, a piebald stallion with feathers in its ears, running wild and free across the plains – with the other horses close up beside him being ridden by his brother and the other braves of his tribe. He could feel the wind tugging at his hair as they galloped faster and faster, chasing the herd of buffalo that were stampeding in a cloud of dust.

"Quick, quick, we must catch them before they reach the river," his brother was calling, and they pounded the sides of their horses with their feet and shouted their hunting cry.

The buffalo were not as fast as the horses, and Abel and his brothers were up alongside them now, with one arm looped through the reins, the other drawing the arrows from their belts and holding them ready to fix in their bows. Then when they were close up beside a big buffalo, Abel's brother gave the signal and they both let go of their reins, and hugging their galloping horses tightly with their knees so that they would not lose their balance, they strung the arrows to their bows and aimed. Whoosh, the arrows went in straight and true, and the huge beast faltered in its stride and stumbled, and then fell with a great thud into the dust. The rest of the herd roared past and disappeared over the hill.

Abel and his brother stopped and leaped down from their horses, turning the buffalo over on its side to look at the size of it. Then they looked at each other. "It is good," said Abel's brother.

"It is good," said Abel. Their lungs were heaving with exhaustion from the chase, and dust had coated the sheen on their bare copper chests, but they knew that they had all that they needed to survive the first weeks of winter. The hide of the buffalo would make them a new teepee and give them warm clothes to keep out the cold; the meat of the buffalo would feed them for a long time to come. They would take it back

and echoed between the high walls of the mountains. And Abel dreamed that all across the plains of America Indian tribes were dancing and singing in honor of the buffalo hunt, and the noise was so great that he sat up in bed and covered his ears with his hands.

Then he opened his eyes. The rain had stopped falling on the roof, and the roaring noise he had heard was of someone parking a truck just outside his window. He went to the window and looked out. His grandfather was climbing down from the truck. There were no teepees and no horses to be seen and there certainly weren't any buffalo. Instead there were cars and tin huts, and maybe a few rabbits to hunt in the bushes.

"Grandfather, I had a dream," said Abel.

"What did you dream?" said the old man.

"I dreamed about what it was like for our people when they had horses and lived in teepees and hunted the buffalo. Long ago, before we wore shirts and trousers, and drove automobiles into town."

Abel's grandfather looked very sad.

"Yes, it was very different then," he said.

"Will you tell me what it was really like to hunt buffalo?" asked Abel.

"I can tell you something of it," said his grandfather, sitting down on Abel's bed.

And when he told him, it was just as Abel had dreamed it.

to the women of the camp, and that night there would be a celebration.

Abel turned over in his sleep, and in his dream there were fires burning in the center of the camp with sparks shooting high from the logs that crackled and spat. And he could smell the sweet mouth-watering smell of the meat roasting on the fire, and could see the shadowy shapes of the women as they moved between the fires, prodding the meat to see if it was cooked. Thump, thump, thump, went the drum, and the feet of the warriors started to pad softly on the ground in time to the drum, the tiny bells jangling on their heels as they moved around and around in a long, weaving line of shining faces and skin gleaming in the firelight.

There was a sound of singing above the beating of the drums and the shuffling of the feet. Louder and louder it grew, faster and faster they danced, so that the sweat poured down their sides and the sounds of their celebration rolled out across the plains where they had hunted the buffalo,

# Claudius the Elephant

Claudius was very sad. It was hard work being a toy elephant when you lived with a little boy like Billy. For Billy was always throwing his toys around, jumping on them, and fighting them. Billy's other toys didn't mind. But, though he was a toy, Claudius could feel things just like a real elephant. And, what's more, he wanted to become a real elephant.

"If only I could live with real elephants," he thought, "I'm sure I would become real, too."

So he ran away. One night when Billy was asleep Claudius rolled to the top of the stairs, then, *bump-bump-bump* he rolled down them. It was a very painful way of getting about, but then toy elephants can't walk, of course, and rolling and falling about were the only ways Claudius could move.

Claudius waited by the door until Billy's father opened it to go to work. Then with a great effort he rolled out of the house, into the street and around the corner.

Claudius felt very tired after all this, so he rolled under a bush and went to sleep. When he woke up he was inside a bag, the bag was inside a car and the car was moving!

The lady driving the car was a teacher and she stopped the car at a school where she worked. She picked up the bag with Claudius inside, and carried it into her classroom.

Claudius became a class toy. He sat on a window-ledge most of the time and watched while the children did their lessons, played games and painted. Very often they painted pictures of Claudius. But, though he was very happy at the school, Claudius still wanted to be real. And when, one day, the teacher told the children about going to a place called a zoo, where there were all kinds of animals, he got very excited.

"If I went to live with the elephants at the zoo," Claudius thought, "I'm sure I could

become real, like them."

So when the day came for the children to go on their trip Claudius rolled off the window-ledge, and *bump-bumped-bumped* his way to the teacher's bag. Then he climbed inside.

Soon they were all at the zoo. It was very large and had lots of different animals. There were lions and monkeys, and zebras, and penguins, and, of course . . . elephants!

The children wondered why all the elephants came lumbering over to be as close to them as they could. But Claudius knew why, and so did the elephants. For they could see his head sticking out of the teacher's bag, and they knew just by looking at him that he was not an ordinary toy.

Claudius knew exactly what to do. He leaned out of the bag so that it fell over, then rolled himself under the fence and toward the deep ditch that separated the visitors from the elephants.

There was a rush of wind, and Claudius landed with a great thud at the bottom.

It was the biggest bump Claudius had ever had. But fortunately no one had seen him.

Well, of course, somebody had seen him – the elephants.

"Are you all right?" one of them asked, peering over the top of the ditch.

"Not bad, thank you," Cladius gasped. "Can you help me up?"

"Not until it gets dark, otherwise someone would see," the elephant answered.

So, after the zoo had closed and all the visitors had gone home, one of the biggest elephants carefully reached his long trunk down and wrapped it around Claudius.

And so Claudius went to live with real elephants at last. Though he never became real himself, all the elephants loved him and carried him around gently in their trunks, and all the baby elephants played with him.

And nobody at the zoo ever knew where Claudius had come from or how he got into the elephants' cage, or why the elephants liked him so much.

# The School's New Wall

The whole class was going to the pottery. There was Jimmy and George and Mickey and Sally and Jill – simply everybody.

The pottery was a very special one because it wasn't in a big smoky town but in the country. And to make it very special indeed it had a playground for children, a zoo, lots of gardens, and shops.

The weather was very bright and clear when the bus arrived to pick them up at their school. They took their lunches with them, and soon they were driving through the country lanes with everyone singing.

Hardly anyone in the class had ever been to a pottery before, so they were all very interested. They watched the clay being mixed and squeezed out – just like toothpaste – to be cut in exactly the right size slices to make cups, and jugs, and pots.

Jill and her brother Paul had been to a pottery before. But at that pottery practically everything had been made by hand, while at this one the things were either shaped by a machine or made by pouring very soft, runny clay into molds and then leaving it to dry and become hard.

The children watched the pottery being made and then baked in a big oven. They saw it being decorated and baked again so that it finished up very hard and covered with beautiful colored patterns and pretty pictures.

After they had seen everything they all went outside to eat their lunches, play in the playground and look at the animals in the zoo.

But George and Mickey went exploring. They walked a long way: past the lake, and past the place for picnics; and then they found a strange thing – a great pile of broken pottery. Cups and bowls and coffee-pots and plates of all different colors, all broken up into little pieces.

"Look at that!" said George.

"Why did they break everything up?" asked Mickey.

"They must be the things that didn't come out right," said George. "Don't you remember they told us about it?"

But Mickey wasn't listening. He'd just had a marvelous idea.

"Come on," he shouted, "let's get back to the others. I've got something to tell them."

For their school was having a new wall built around the playground, facing the street. And their teacher had told them to try to think of a way of decorating it themselves.

Everyone had been asked to think up suggestions.

That was Mickey's idea. He had thought of a way of using the broken pottery, and when he told the others about it they all agreed it was the best idea any of them had had.

So they told the teacher. And he thought it was a wonderful idea too. So did the headmaster when the teacher told *him*.

They put cement over the bricks of the wall, and while it was still wet, they stuck in pieces of broken pottery.

They made rows of red and yellow and green stripes along the bottom, then a big area in the middle of all different colours and shapes mixed, then wavy lines of pink and brown with big circles of yellow. At the top they put more lines of black and green and white.

It looked wonderful, and people came from miles around to watch the children working at it. When it was finished they all went on television and had their pictures in the newspaper.

They made the gayest, brightest, prettiest wall in all the town. For it sparkled in the summer sun and still looked bright and cheerful in the cold dark weather of winter.

# Crybaby Hilda and the Magic Flower

Hilda was a sad girl. She was always crying over something or other. In fact, she was really an awful crybaby.

One day she was playing in her garden when a lovely butterfly flew in.

Hilda had never seen anything so lovely. Its wings shone like a rainbow – sometimes blue and sometimes green – with black and golden frills around the edges. She reached out to pick him up.

"Tut tut, mustn't touch!" said the butterfly. He fluttered out of reach.

"But I only want to know if you feel as pretty as you look!" said Hilda. "I just want to touch your wings."

"Not a chance!" he squeaked. "Why, a great big creature like you is too clumsy for a little fellow like me."

"I'm *not* a great big creature!" shouted

Hilda. She was quite annoyed at being called a creature, big or small. But the butterfly laughed at her.

"From where I'm sitting," he said saucily, "you look like a great big creature. You shan't touch me!" He sprang into the air.

Hilda didn't like being laughed at, even by a butterfly. She tried to grab him from the air. He laughed – a little butterfly titter it was – and skittered away. Hilda chased after him.

Round and round the garden they went, with the butterfly skittering and tittering and Hilda shouting and grabbing.

At last the butterfly grew tired of the game. So he flew away over the wall and Hilda never saw him again.

I guess you know what crybaby Hilda did then? That's right. She sat down on the grass and started bawling. She cried and cried until the tears poured down her face and dripped from her chin.

And then she felt more tears falling – right on top of her head!

Hilda looked up and there was a droopy blue flower, looking very sad indeed. It was crying all over her. Hilda didn't like that one bit. You see, flower tears are made of nectar, and are very sticky.

"Stop dripping on my hair, you ugly old flower," snapped Hilda.

"I'm sorry," sobbed the flower, "but I can't help crying. You make me do it."

"Are you crying because I'm crying?" Hilda asked.

The flower nodded.

"If I stop crying, will you stop too?" she asked.

The flower nodded again. So Hilda stopped crying. Right away the flower stopped crying too. It lifted up its head, and turned from blue to red. Then it wasn't ugly any more, but beautiful.

It was really a magic flower! After that, every time Hilda cried, she went to look at the flower. Sure enough, it would be crying too. It looked so sad and miserable that Hilda had to stop crying, so it could stop crying too.

Hilda decided to give up crying altogether, because she didn't want to make her magic flower unhappy. Soon she'd completely forgotten how to cry, and no one called her a crybaby any more.

Why, she didn't even cry when the flower died. Its petals withered and drooped, and fell away. Just a little brown lump was left on the end of its stem.

Every day Hilda went to look at the lump, hoping the flower would come back. Every day the lump was bigger. Then, one day, it went POP! Out flew hundreds and hundreds of tiny black seeds, riding on fluffy white parachutes. The wind blew them everywhere. Most of them landed in Hilda's garden, but some flew over the wall.

Then it was wintertime, the long, cold wintertime. Nothing happened in Hilda's garden. But then spring came along. All the seeds sprouted, and grew up into big plants. Soon every one of them burst into bloom, and Hilda's garden was full of beautiful red magic flowers!

No one knows where Hilda's garden is, so you can't go to see her flowers. But some of those seeds blew over the wall, remember? Did they land in your garden?

# Dylan Dragon

Dylan dragon lived in a cave in a Welsh mountain. He lived there because he was a Welsh dragon.

His cave was leaky and lonely. The damp wasn't too bad, because he could always steam the walls dry by breathing fire on them. But the loneliness was terrible.

You see, Dylan was a friendly dragon. He wanted company. But nobody wanted him. The truth is, he frightened people.

There was a nice-looking village in a nearby valley. Dylan liked to look down at it and watch the children playing.

Once he went to the village to play with the children. But they were frightened and ran from him. Then the grown-ups shouted at him, and chased him with big sticks. Poor Dylan was frightened then. He scooted back to his cave and never dared go near the village again.

But one day there was a great storm. Black clouds filled the sky and settled on the mountains. They grumbled and thundered and threw lightning bolts.

High on his mountain, Dylan was in the thick of it. He was terribly frightened. He huddled at the back of his cave. Every time the thunder boomed, the whole cave jumped. Every time the lightning flashed, poor Dylan dragon jumped with fright. Then the rain poured down. The cave leaked, and Dylan was soon soaked right through.

Then there came such a clap of thunder, and such a bolt of lightning, that the whole mountain shook. Dylan shook so hard, all his pointed teeth rattled together. The cave roof began to fall down. Dylan ran out – just in time. Behind him, the whole cave collapsed into a pile of rubble.

Dylan was so scared, he ran straight down the mountain. When he stopped, he found himself in the middle of the village. And it was flooded from the rain. He was up to his knees in water!

"I must help the villagers," he said, even though they frightened him.

He dashed to the nearest house and pounded on the door. "Come out quick," he called, "before the flood rises more!"

He made such a row, everyone looked from their windows. What a fright they had! All around them was the swirling flood-water. And in it was a horrible-looking brown dragon! No one would come out. They didn't like the look of Dylan.

"I see I'll have to *make* them come out," thought Dylan. And with that he rushed to an open window, where a small boy was peeping out at him. Dylan seized the boy's collar in his great mouth. He dragged him through the window and ran off with him.

Everyone was afraid that Dylan meant to eat the boy. They all chased after him. Of course that was just what Dylan wanted. He ran and ran till he reached a hill above the flood. Then he put down the boy (he wasn't a bit hurt) and waited for the others.

"Don't hit him!" cried the boy as they rushed at Dylan with sticks and stones. "He only wanted to save us!"

Everyone turned to look back at the village. The water was half over the houses by then. "You *have* saved us," they told Dylan. "And we're grateful to you, even if you are an ugly dragon!"

There was a big barn on the hill. They all went inside, taking Dylan with them. Then he frightened them all over again – he started spouting flame!

The boy was the only one who wasn't afraid. He stood close to Dylan, warming himself as the flame huffed and puffed. At last the others crept closer to Dylan. Soon they were all warm and dry.

And then a marvelous thing happened. All the brown color flaked away from Dylan. It wasn't his color at all. It was mud. His real coat was green and gold and brilliant blue, and very beautiful.

"Why, he's lovely!" said everyone. Soon they were good friends, and Dylan never frightened them again.

When the flood went down, they took Dylan back to the village. They built him a house – a special dragon house – and Dylan lived happily there forever after.

# The Wonderful Jug of Cream

Long, long ago, in France, in the days before money was invented, a little boy called Gaston lived with his father and mother and his sister Yvette in a little house. It was made of wood and mud mixed with straw and it stood in a clearing in a great forest.

Gaston's mother and father kept a herd of cows which gave lots of milk. Gaston and his sister drank lots of milk, but most of all they loved the thick cream that rose to the top.

But one day, Gaston's mother said: "We have more milk and cream than we need for ourselves, so I want you and Yvette to take a jug each to the village and exchange them for something for the house."

So Gaston and Yvette picked up two of the biggest jugs, one full of milk, the other of cream. They plugged them with big pieces of cork, and set out.

Now they had a long way to go and it was a very hot day. So when the two children reached the top of the hill overlooking the village they decided to sit down for a rest.

But as Gaston put his jug down he tripped and fell. The jug toppled over on to its side and began rolling down the hill. Gaston raced after the jug as fast as he could, but he couldn't catch it. In fact, nothing and nobody could stop that jug until it broke in pieces, with a great crash, against the door of the house that belonged to Charles, the most important man in the village. Now Charles also enjoyed eating and drinking more than anyone in the village.

So he was very interested in Gaston's jug – not for the cream inside (he had plenty of his own); but when the jug had smashed into pieces no cream had run out. So if the cream hadn't run out when the jug had broken, or on the way down the hill, where had it gone?

Charles and Gaston looked at the bottom half of the jug which had stayed in one big piece.

There *was* something inside. But it wasn't

cream. It was soft but firm, and pale yellow. Charles smelled it. It smelled good. Then he and Gaston tasted it. It tasted even better. It was butter – the first butter anyone had ever made or ever tasted.

Charles took all the wonderful new food that Gaston had invented. In return he gave him a little knife for himself, a comb and some needles for his mother and as much fine woolen cloth as he could carry.

Gaston went home feeling very excited. But everyone at home was excited, too, even before Gaston told them about his invention.

"I invented a new . . . " he began.

"Your sister invented . . . " started his mother.

". . . a new . . ." Gaston tried again. But everyone was talking at once.

"FOOD," they all said together.

"Yes, yes, Yvette invented a new food!"

"No," said Gaston, "I invented it."

"But the jug of milk changed," said Father.

"You mean the *cream*. It changed when it rolled down the hill."

"No, no, no," shouted Yvette. "The *milk* changed when I left it in the sun."

For, while Gaston had been chasing his jug down the hill, Yvette had fallen asleep and left the milk standing in the sun.

"When I woke up it was late," she said, "so I went straight home. But when I opened the jug the milk had a funny smell. And some of it was very thick and the rest was all watery. So I drained off the water and hung the rest in a clean cloth to drain some more – "

"And I added some salt," said Mother.

" – and now we've got this," went on Yvette, showing Gaston a dish full of something smooth and white like cream, but also thick and with a sharp, delicious taste.

For while Gaston had been inventing butter, Yvette had invented cheese!

# The White Peacock

In the grounds of the palace in the city of Lisbon there lived a white peacock. He was very beautiful and he was the only white peacock in the world. Every day he strutted about the palace gardens, spreading his tail for all to see and admiring his reflection in the waters of the goldfish pond. The other peacocks, although they were very beautiful and had lovely blue and green tails, were very jealous of the white peacock because he attracted so much attention and people came from far and wide to look at him. The white peacock became more and more famous, and as a result he grew more and more boastful.

One day in the middle of the hot summer, the fat Queen was looking out of the windows of the palace and wishing she knew some way of staying cool. Her royal dresses were heavy and thick, and her face was red from the heat. As she leaned on the window-sill she saw the white peacock parading around the gardens, spreading his wonderful tail to the world, and she felt very angry that all her subjects should come to gaze at him, who was so smart and cool, and never to look at her, who was so heavy and hot. Suddenly a very clever thought struck her. "That peacock needs to be taught a lesson," she said to herself, and she summoned the gardener.

"Tomorrow," she said, "is Midsummer's Day, and the King is holding a Ball in the palace. All the Kings and Queens of Europe will be there, and their most important ministers. You understand of course that I have to look my very best. I must have

the tail of that white peacock to use as a fan."

"Yes ma'am," said the gardener, backing out of the door. He hurried out of the palace and down the steps into the gardens, and gathered all the blue and green peacocks around him, and told them what the Queen had said. They thought it was the most wonderful idea, and they clutched their feathers and rolled about with laughter.

Then the gardener said to the white peacock: "You had better make the most of that tail because tomorrow you won't have it anymore. Tomorrow night that tail of yours which you think is so fancy will be keeping the heat off Her Majesty's face. I shall be coming for you with my shears and cutting off those long white tail feathers to make the most beautiful fan that has ever been held in the hand of a Queen."

And then an extraordinary thing happened. The white peacock sank down on to his stomach, and closed up his beautiful white tail, so that he looked small and ordinary, like a tired white chicken, and a large gold tear fell from each of his eyes onto the green grass. Everyone gazed in astonishment, for nobody had ever seen the white peacock look miserable.

After what seemed like a very long time, the white peacock stood up and began to walk very slowly and sadly towards the palace, his lovely white tail dragging on the ground behind him and getting covered with earth and twigs. Up the steps of the palace he went, past the footmen at the great doors, and into the Queen's drawing-room where he stopped before her throne.

"Your Majesty," he said in a small cracked voice, "what must I do to keep my beautiful tail?" And a large gold tear fell on to the Queen's slipper.

The Queen, who had watched all that had happened from the window and was really a very kind queen, could not help feeling sorry for the white peacock and decided that he had learned his lesson. So she said, "You may keep your tail on one condition. Whenever I call you, you must come and wave your tail back and forth in front of my face so that I stay cool on the hottest of days. Furthermore," said the Queen, "you can start your duties tomorrow by fanning me at the Midsummer Ball."

The peacock bowed very low, and said he would be honored to serve Her Majesty in this way, and he said, too, that he would never again strut about the palace grounds as if he were the only peacock in the world (even if he was the only white one, he added, slightly under his breath).

So the next night, in front of the Kings and Queens of Europe, and their most important ministers, the white peacock waved his beautiful tail gently to and fro beside the Queen's throne. And the Queen looked cool and slim and lovely because the peacock's tail had fanned away her hotness and her fatness. She was very happy, and so were the people of Lisbon, because they could still come and see their beautiful white peacock spread his tail in the gardens of the palace.

# The Island of Treasure

Once, in the great city of Antwerp, in Belgium, there lived a little boy called Dieter. There have always been lots of jewelers in Antwerp, and Dieter loved to watch them at work. Or he did until one night he had a dream. He dreamed of the most marvelous rings, necklaces and bracelets, and beautiful cups and bowls of shining silver and gold.

Dieter searched the whole of Antwerp, but nowhere could he find any jewelry so beautiful.

He became a sailor. But even though he traveled all over the world, he never managed to find anything to equal the jewelry in his dream.

Then, one day, during a terrible storm, an enormous wave came right over Dieter's ship and swept him into the sea. He cried for help, but no one could hear him over the roar of the waves and the scream of the wind. He swam for many hours, until another great wave caught him and tossed him up onto the beach of a tiny island.

Well, Dieter was too tired to care where he was, and so, after crawling a little way further up the beach to be safe from the tide, he fell asleep.

When he awoke the sun was shining brightly. And on such a scene!

For the little island was like no other island Dieter had ever heard of. The beach didn't have sand or pebbles. It was made up entirely of *rings*: gold rings, silver rings, rings with all kinds of precious stones.

Dieter could hardly believe his eyes. At last his dream had come true. All around him, the loveliest jewelry shone and glittered in the sunshine. Further up the beach, just as if they had been washed up by the tide, lay dazzling mounds of necklaces and bracelets. And further up still were even bigger things – cups and plates and bowls, in silver and gold.

Dieter collected some of the biggest bowls he could find and filled them with as many rings and bracelets and necklaces as he could. Then he wrapped everything up in his shirt and sat down for a rest.

But soon the wind started to howl again, and suddenly an enormous wave broke right over the top of the island. Once again Dieter was swept away.

The wave seemed to carry him for miles and miles before dropping him right back on the deck of a ship again – the deck of his own ship!

Dieter stumbled below to where the other sailors were sitting.

"Dieter, you've been on deck," someone said. "You should be careful – it's easy to get washed overboard in weather like this."

"But I *have* been washed overboard," Dieter replied. "It happened yesterday. I was washed up on an island, got carried away again today, and somehow ended up back on this ship."

"What are you talking about?" a sailor said. "There wasn't any storm yesterday. And I saw you go on deck a few minutes ago – you've been dreaming!"

Dieter couldn't believe his ears. And he still had his bundle of treasure. So he found a quiet place by himself to unwrap it, and sure enough, the wonderful jewelry was still there! He hadn't been dreaming!

Dieter took his treasure back home to Antwerp and became the most famous jeweler and goldsmith in the whole of Belgium.

Since Dieter's time, hundreds of other people have tried to find his island of treasure. But no one ever has. From that day to this.

# Vanessa the Vain Mermaid

Vanessa was a beautiful mermaid. She lived, with many mermaids and mermen, at the Merhome in the soft warm sea.

Vanessa wasn't happy. She had no friends, because she was too vain about her beauty. The mermaids didn't like her because she was always rudely telling them how ugly they were, compared to her. The mermen didn't like her because she was always upsetting the other mermaids.

Poor, silly, unhappy mermaid.

One day Vanessa left the Merhome. "As I have no friends, I shall be better off on my own," she thought.

She swam far from the Merhome, to the oyster sea where the giant octopus lived. There she spent half her days hunting for oyster pearls to deck herself. The other half she spent combing her long black hair and admiring herself in a mirror.

One day, as she was looking for pearls, she heard the dreadful sound of shark voices! Very slowly and carefully she crept into a thicket of anemones, the beautiful flowers of the sea. She listened to two sharks talking.

Said the first shark: "I've just found a place full of mermaids and mermen!"

Said the second shark: "Ha-ha-heee! Let's have a feast of delicious merpeople!"

But the first shark said: "Wait a bit. I have an idea. Let's find some more sharks. Then we can catch every last mermaid and merman!"

The second shark agreed.

From her hiding place, Vanessa heard every evil word! She waited until the sharks had gone off for their fellows. Then she headed for the Merhome. She had to warn her people of the terrible danger.

In her hurry, she swam too close to a sea urchin. Its spines stuck out and scratched her. She cried out in pain.

Though they were already swimming away, the sharks heard the mermaid's voice. They came rushing back.

When Vanessa saw them diving at her, with red eyes blazing and sharp teeth gaping, she fled. But sharks are faster

than mermaids. They were snapping at her tail when she flashed out of reach into a little cave in a coral reef.

The sharks snarled and whined outside the cave, unable to reach her. At last one left, to call other sharks for the attack on the Merhome. The second shark stayed in front of the cave.

At first Vanessa, trapped in the cave, cried bitterly in fear for herself and the merpeople. Then she saw a small entrance at the back of the cave. It looked too small for her. But she tried to wriggle through. She pushed and struggled. The sharp coral tugged the pearls from her hair. It tore the frill on her pretty tail. But this time she didn't make any sound at all, though it hurt her.

Finally she slipped free. The guard shark didn't see her drifting silently away. When she was out of sight, she dashed through the sea, but not to the Merhome. She rushed straight to the lair of the giant octopus!

Suddenly a long octopus tentacle grabbed her, and a bubbly voice said: "So! Here's a pretty thing. You're lucky I doesn't eat mermaids. I only likes oysters!"

"But you like eating sharks too, don't you?" asked clever Vanessa.

"I does, I does!" burbled the octopus. "When I can catch 'em!"

"Then come with me, and you shall have more sharks than you've ever seen before," she promised.

She streaked away to the Merhome, with the great octopus wallowing behind her as fast as he could wallow.

They reached the Merhome and gave the warning just in time. Even as the mermen were seizing their sharp trident spears, the sharks poured in.

A terrible battle was fought that day. But the mermen and the octopus were victorious. Not one shark escaped them.

Then Vanessa was a great heroine, and all the merpeople became her friends. She was never again vain or rude, so she stayed friends with everyone in the Merhome.

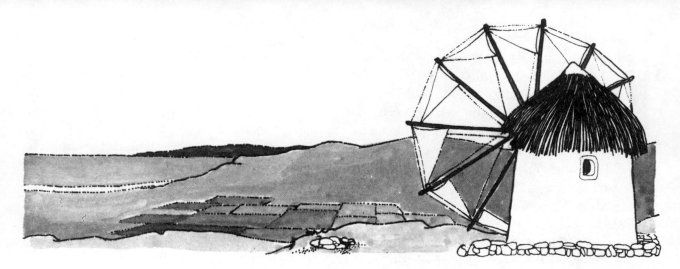

# The Little Windmill That Went Traveling

Zito was a little windmill who lived on the top of a hill in Portugal. The hill was smooth and round and at the bottom were fields of wheat and corn and all kinds of fruit.

But Zito wasn't satisfied. Most people thought he was very important – the miller who owned him did, so did the farmers who brought their wheat to him to be made into flour. But the doctor had a clever daughter and, one day, Zito overheard her telling the miller about the windmills in a country called Holland.

"Zito is so small," she said, "but in Holland the windmills are big and strong, and have great wide arms to catch the wind with. Not thin little arms like Zito's."

Zito hadn't liked that at all. Neither had the miller.

"That may be so," the miller had replied, "but Zito works very well. And, you see, he has little whistles along his arms which sing in the wind and point in different directions. So if the wind blows from another way they play a different note to tell me to turn Zito's arms to face the wind again. I'm sure Dutch windmills don't have that!"

Well, they had gone on arguing, and the doctor's daughter had finally admitted that Zito worked very well and looked very pretty too.

But Zito was still offended.

He thought about it all that day, and the next. He just couldn't forget about those big, powerful windmills in Holland.

Now windmills, of course, are very friendly with the wind, and so Zito told it everything the doctor's daughter had said.

"I want to see those big foreign windmills myself," Zito said.

"Well, that isn't too difficult," replied the wind, "you can dream about them the next time I'm blowing from the south."

Some days passed, then, finally, the wind started to blow from the south and toward the north.

"I'm going to Holland, I'm going to Holland," Zito whistled happily. He had never been so excited. In fact he was so excited that it took him a long time to fall asleep.

But when at last he did, he dreamed he was flying on the wind far, far to the north. On the way they passed over Spain, and France, and Belgium, until, at last, they came to Holland.

In front of him he saw a whole row of

windmills. They were much bigger than he was, just as the doctor's daughter had said. And they really did have big wide arms, which creaked and clanked as they turned.

Zito was very impressed.

"Hallo there," he said to the first windmill, "my name is Zito – which is Portuguese for small. Do you understand Portuguese?"

"No," replied the Dutch windmill, "and you don't speak Dutch. But since this is a dream we can understand what each of us is *thinking*, and that's the important thing. My name is Zan."

"How big you are, Zan," said Zito. "You must grind lots of flour."

"Oh no, none at all," answered Zan, "I pump water – nearly all Dutch windmills do."

Now Zito thought that sounded very dull, but he was too polite to say so. So he asked: "Well, what's the weather like here?"

"We have a lot of rain," Zan replied, "the wind is very strong, and the winters are cold and dark."

Zito didn't like the sound of that at all. So he said goodbye to Zan and asked the wind to fly him home.

For a moment Zito felt himself flying through the air. Then he awoke with a start. The sun was just rising over the top of the hills, and he could see the ripe grapes in the fields, the wheat, the corn, and fruit trees.

"I don't care if I am small," Zito said to himself. "I like it here and I like being the way I am."

# The Saucy Monkey and the Good Giraffe

A saucy monkey named Sid lived in an acacia tree. One day he was sitting there, admiring the blossoms, when a young giraffe ambled up. The giraffe's name was Bert.

Without a "by your leave," young Bert started eating the leaves. The whole tree jerked and swayed. Sid held on to a branch to keep himself from falling out.

"Stop eating my tree, you long-necked creature!" shouted saucy Sid.

Young Bert looked up at Sid. He wasn't annoyed at being called long-necked, because he was. But he didn't like being called a creature. So he said, "Dear, dear, you long-tailed creature. You don't eat acacia leaves, do you?"

"No," said Sid.

"Well, I do," said Bert. And he went right on chewing up Sid's leaves.

That made Sid angry. He pulled fistfuls of lovely, fluffy yellow flowers from the tree and hurled them at Bert.

The flowers didn't hurt Bert, but they annoyed him. He said: "I see I must teach you a lesson, you saucy monkey!"

And with that, he reached out his long black tongue and grabbed Sid. He pulled Sid clear out of the tree and flipped him over his head! Sid fell on Bert's long neck. He slid right down it and landed with a thump on Bert's back.

104

Sid was very surprised, very *very* scared, and very very *very* annoyed. He wanted to jump down from Bert's back, but it was a long way down to the ground. So he jumped up and down. He pounded with his little fists (which didn't hurt young Bert a bit) and bawled.

"Dear, dear, you are hot-tempered," said Bert. "You need cooling down." And he set off through the trees at a run.

He ran straight to a water hole, with Sid hanging on for dear life. Bert tipped his head down to the water.

Caught by surprise, Sid shot down Bert's neck. He slid from one end to the other, and bumped into Bert's soft little horns. He somersaulted between Bert's ears, and splashed into the water hole.

Bert quickly reached out with his long black tongue and hauled him out again.

Sid stood, drenched and dripping, on the bank. He wasn't angry any more, but he was surprised. "Why did you dunk me in the water hole?" he asked.

"To cool your temper," Bert replied.

Sid thought of that for a bit. Then he said, "You're right. I was being silly. There are lots of trees, but you're the only giraffe I know. Let's be friends!"

Bert agreed at once, and they were friends. They went everywhere together, with Sid riding on Bert's back.

But, early one morning, a trapper came to their land. While Bert was dozing under a tree, Sid wandered off to look at this strange new creature. The man promptly caught him and put him in a wooden cage.

He put the cage in the back of his truck.

"From now on you'll live in a zoo," he told Sid. Then he climbed into the truck and drove off.

Sid didn't want to leave Bert and live in a zoo. He wailed for help.

Alert Bert, hearing the cry, woke at once. He soon saw what had happened, and he chased after the truck.

Like all giraffes, he was a fast runner. He caught up with the truck easily. Running alongside, he reached his long neck over the side. He scooped out Sid, little cage and all. Then he cantered off, with the cage swinging from his mouth.

The trapper never even noticed what had happened. He was most surprised when he discovered Sid was gone, cage and all. He's still wondering what happened.

I suppose you're wondering how Sid got out of the cage? The answer's simple – Bert opened the latch with his clever tongue. Out popped Sid, not the least bit hurt by his latest adventure.

After that the good giraffe and the saucy monkey had many more adventures, but they were never parted again.

# Little Lost Whale

Young Wilbur was a whale. He lived with his mother in the deep sea. One day, when he went to the surface for a breath of air, Wilbur saw the land. He thought it was a huge whale floating on the sea. It gave him an awful fright, and he dove back to his mother. "There's a huge whale up there!" he cried.

His mother laughed. "That's no whale," she said. "That's the land!"

She told him about the land and the people who lived on it. "Most of them are quite nice, I suppose," she said. "But some are our enemies. They're the ones who come out in boats and try to catch us!"

Wilbur shivered with fright. He'd once been chased by a whaling ship, and that was awful to remember.

"So, young Wilbur," his mother said, "steer clear of the land, or the whaler men may catch you!"

But, one foggy day, when he couldn't see his fin before his face, Wilbur came to the land without knowing it. You see, he came across a strange current of water. It tasted different than sea water. Wilbur was curious, so he swam up the current.

Being such a young whale, Wilbur didn't realize it was river water he was tasting. He swam on and on, until the fog quite suddenly lifted. He looked around. Disaster! There was land on both sides of him, closer than he'd ever seen before. He had swum right up the river!

Standing on the bank was a strange creature. "That must be a man," thought Wilbur. "I'd better get out of here, fast! Before he throws a harpoon at me!"

Just then the man shouted and pointed at him. Soon there were hundreds of people on the bank, all gaping at Wilbur.

"A whale! A whale!" they cried.

Wilbur panicked. He dove to the bottom and swam off as fast as he could. But he was swimming *up* the river!

He dashed on till he came to a place where the water ran fast and furious. Wilbur thought he was coming back to the sea. Poor fellow, he'd never heard of a weir. He was in the rough water below a weir (which is a kind of dam, with water running over its top).

Wilbur swam into the weir. He was going so fast, he crashed right over, and landed in the deep pool above it. The crash made him stop and think. He soon realized he should swim *down* the river to reach the sea. But when he tried, he couldn't get past the weir. He was trapped!

Poor Wilbur sank to the bottom of the pool, lonely and frightened. At last he had to come up for air. But, as he surfaced, he felt a bump on his back.

Then a voice called from right above him: "Let me down!"

Wilbur looked up. On his back was a rowboat. In it was Sam, the lock-keeper.

"Don't be afraid," said Sam. "I've come to help you out of this mess."

"You're not trying to catch me, are you?" asked frightened Wilbur.

"No, no! We all want to see you get free," said Sam. He pointed to the bank, where hundreds of people stood watching them. "They're all your friends," said Sam.

Wilbur was very pleased. So he sank gently down until Sam's boat floated from his back. Then he surfaced again.

"How can I get out?" he asked. "I want to go back to my mother and the sea."

Sam told him. Then he rowed ashore.

Wilbur did just as Sam had told him. He swam around the pool, faster and faster, till he was zooming like a speedboat. Then he made a huge leap, clear over the weir, and landed on the downstream side.

He made such a great splash, he soaked all the people on the bank. But they didn't mind. They cheered because he was free.

Wilbur smiled at his friends. He spouted a tall white fountain of water to show them how happy he was.

"Thar she blows!" shouted the people. They laughed and clapped and waved to Wilbur. Everyone loved the little whale.

Wilbur waved his tail to Sam. Then he swam away down the river, and didn't stop till he reached the deep sea.

# Septimus Sebastian Fry's Tricycle

When Septimus Sebastian Fry was a boy, he had a tricycle. When he was a young man, he had a bicycle. But when he became an old man, he made himself a new tricycle.

Sep (everyone called him Sep) made his new tricycle because he liked surprising people. All his friends and neighbors knew he was making it. Well, not quite. They knew he was making something, but they didn't know what it was.

Every morning, after his breakfast of cornflakes and honey, Sep went to his garage. Soon interesting sounds of forging, hammering and drilling came from it.

Everyone wondered what those interesting sounds meant. They asked Sep.

Old Sep just grinned and winked. "You wait and see. All in good time, you shall see," he said.

So they waited to see what old Sep was up to. But one old neighbor, Mrs. Quest, couldn't hold her curiosity. One day, when fascinating buzzing and tinkling sounds poured from the garage, she could wait no longer. She just *had* to see. So she crept through Sep's gate. She sidled past the house. She tiptoed up to the garage. She peeked in at the window and . . .

"Yeep!" yelped Mrs. Quest. On the other side of the glass, one inch from her nose, was old Sep. He was making a horrible, frightening face at her!

Clever old Sep had seen her coming! She never saw his tricycle. She scooted from the garage, past the house and hopped right over the gate. Yes she did, and how funny she looked! Old Sep had to laugh.

But after a while he stopped laughing. He began to feel ashamed of what he had done. "Septimus Sebastian Fry," he said to himself, "that was a wrong thing to do. You shouldn't frighten people, even if they are nosy!"

By the time he'd finished giving himself a good talking-to, Sep was very sorry for what he'd done. "I shall do something nice, to show her I'm sorry," he said.

Do you know what he did? He took apart the tricycle – which was almost finished – and built it all over again. He worked very hard and very long. Sep was so busy, his friends hardly saw him from one week's end to the next.

Mrs. Quest was also ashamed of herself, for letting her curiosity run away with her. She wished she could think of some way to show old Sep she was sorry.

Then, one bright sunshiny morning, Sep came from his house all dressed up in his best clothes. He wore his tight blue suit and his fancy brown and white shoes. His tie was bright red silk, and his hat was dapper straw.

Sep marched to his garage. He threw the doors wide open. He hopped inside and came back out – on his tricycle! It was finished at last.

What a beauty it was! It was big, of course, three times as big as an ordinary tricycle. It was painted in gleaming gold. It had a sunshade with a fringe on top. It had pedals, but it also had a little motor at the back, for zipping up hills comfortably. It had a big picnic basket, a shiny mirror, and many more gadgets for this and that. For a horn, it had a big brass tuba on the handlebars!

And it had two comfortable seats, one beside the other!

Old Sep pedaled up to Mrs. Quest's door. Out popped Mrs. Quest. She was so excited, she didn't know what to do. She thought the tricycle was quite wonderful.

"Good morning, dear Mrs. Quest," said old Sep, politely raising his hat. "Please forgive my bad manners of the past. I would be delighted if you would come for a little spin on my machine. As you can see, it's specially built for two!"

Mrs. Quest was thrilled. "I shall come if you will also forgive my bad manners of the past," she replied.

"Let's forget the past," said Sep.

So Mrs. Quest put on her best coat and hat, and her fancy lace gloves.

Then they pedaled away on the tricycle, happy friends for evermore.

# The Tea-Spaniel

The Hotel Splendiferous was certainly the most expensive hotel in town. There were thick soft carpets on the floors and huge sparkling chandeliers hanging from the ceilings. Only the very richest people could afford to stay there. Every day, between 4 o'clock and 5 o'clock, afternoon tea was served in the dining room. The generals and the earls and the politicians and the fat duchesses would get up from their after-lunch naps or their games of bridge and would sit down at their tables in the dining room to be served with tea. Alfonso, the head waiter, would sweep in and out, taking their orders for cakes and scones, and making sure that everything was exactly as it should be in the most expensive hotel in town. There was never any noise in the dining room except the soft clinking of cups and a gentle murmur of voices. It was a terribly respectable place.

One afternoon Alfonso was busying himself with the orders of the guests when an unheard-of thing happened. A voice hailed him very loudly across the room.

"I say, waiter, what about my tea?"

Everyone turned around in astonishment. Who had dared to behave so badly? And when they saw who it was they nearly fell off their chairs in horror. Alfonso's eyebrows shot up into his hair. What on earth was this? There, sitting at the corner table by the window, with his paws on the table-cloth and a napkin tied around his neck, was a Springer spaniel with a singularly sassy expression. Alfonso gathered himself together and stormed across to demand the meaning of this.

"And just who do you think you are?" he inquired of the spaniel.

"Oh, good afternoon, I'm glad you've come at last," said the spaniel. "Now I would like to order –"

"I asked you who you were," interrupted Alfonso.

"Oh, don't you know? I'm the Tea-

Alfonso had had enough. He had never before been treated in such a way by a guest at the Hotel Splendiferous, and he wasn't going to be ordered about by a sassy spaniel. He strode away across the dining room to look after the other guests.

"BOW WOW WOOF!" The most deafening barks came from the corner table. The chandelier in the center of the room tinkled and shook, the guests dropped their monocles and the fat duchesses ran from the room, complaining that they had never seen such preposterous behavior at the hotel before. The Tea-Spaniel was standing on the table making very sure that everyone heard what he had to say.

"BOW WOW WOOF! I want a plate of buttered toast, WOOF, three slices of sponge cake, BOW WOW, some chocolate biscuits, WOOF, as many meringues as you can find, and a large bowl of water. WOOF! Also some grapes, peeled if you please," he added.

Then he went on barking until Alfonso and several other waiters came back from the kitchen with his order. By now all the guests had fled from the noise.

"Will you kindly stop making that awful racket!" shouted Alfonso, still trembling with indignation.

"Yes certainly," said the Tea-Spaniel, "now that you've brought me my tea. And in future I hope you will remember that it isn't just generals and duchesses who get hungry at 4 o'clock."

And with that he settled down to enjoy himself immensely.

Spaniel," said the Tea-Spaniel. "I'm pretty well-known about town because I like to take tea in all the best places. As it's Sunday I thought I would come to the best place of all."

"But I can't serve you. You're a spaniel," said Alfonso. "I only serve generals and duchesses and suchlike. You shouldn't really have been allowed to get in here at all."

"Don't be such a snob," said the Tea-Spaniel. "Everyone else serves me tea, and in any case I'm a very respectable and well-bred spaniel. But I warn you I shall start to behave very badly indeed if you don't bring me my tea."

"Oh yes, and what will you do?" said Alfonso, who was still feeling very annoyed at having to wait on a dog.

"I shall bark," said the Tea-Spaniel, "and I shall go on barking until something happens."

# The Enchanted
# Bird of Beauty

The Bird of Beauty lived in a dark, wet forest. Among the twisted, leafless trees his lonely song rang out. But no one heard it. The forest was enchanted by an evil witch, and people never dared go there.

He was a beautiful bird. He stood as tall as a man. His feathers, of many colors, glowed in his long tail, on his great wings, and on his proud head.

One day his sad song soared up, telling the dim sky and the dead trees of his loneliness. He sang of heartbreak and despair, but even so his song was lovely.

But, this day, his song was heard. Through the trees, stumbling and crying, came a poor ugly girl. She was lost, and cold, and shivering. When she saw the bird, she smiled sweetly.

But the bird cried out: "Run away!"

"Why?" she called back. "You and your song are beautiful, and I am lost in this terrible place."

"Beautiful I may be," replied the bird, "but I am terrible too. The witch has enchanted me, and put me here to catch poor wanderers like yourself. She will change you to another form, and keep you here like me. I know, for I was once a man."

At that the girl cried aloud. "But why don't you fly away?" she asked.

"I cannot," said the bird. Then she saw his chain. It was a great silver chain, and it held his foot to the tree.

"I will help you, poor bird," said the girl. She seized a stone and beat it against the chain. Suddenly it fell apart.

The bird sighed a great sigh, and flapped his wings. "How can I thank you?" he asked. "How can I repay you for my freedom?" Then he saw that the girl, in her thin, torn dress, was still shivering. "My feathers shall make a cloak for you!"

He quickly pulled all the lovely feathers from his wings and tail. He tied them into a rainbow cloak and put it around her.

At once she was warm. The cloak hung to the ground. The collar stood in a great ruff, higher than her head.

Nearby was a deep, still pool. She walked to it, and looked at her reflection. "Why, I'm beautiful now!" she said.

Suddenly there came a crashing noise. Before the girl could move, the wicked witch stood before her. "How did you lose your chain? Who is here? I heard voices!" screamed the witch.

From those words, the girl knew that the witch thought *she* was the bird! She huddled in the cloak and whispered meekly: "I was talking to a bird."

"You lie!" the witch screeched. "For that, I shall turn you into a toad!"

As she spoke, she pointed her magic wand. The girl screamed and tried to run, but she tripped on her cloak and fell.

"Toad! Toad! Forever be a toad!" chanted the witch. But her wand now pointed at her own reflection in the pool, and she bewitched herself! In an instant she was a nasty, warty little toad. The wand fell, and the bird flew out and seized it.

"Evil magic, depart forever!" he cried.

At that, the witch toad fell into the pond like a stone, and was never seen again. The trees sprang straight, and green leaves covered their branches. And although the leaves almost hid the sky, the forest grew brighter. Even the dismal mists departed, and the sun shone.

The wand crumbled to harmless dust. The

bird gave a great cry of joy. Then he looked at the girl, and he cried in sorrow. "Look," he wept, "you are now truly a bird. What have I done to you?"

She looked into the pond and saw that she was indeed a bird. Then she laughed in great happiness. "But how wonderful!" she said. "Once I was an ugly girl, but now I am as beautiful as you."

She spoke true. For she was covered in lacy fine feathers, even as he was.

From that day the forest has been enchanted in endless beauty. People go there to revel in its loveliness. Sometimes they hear the haunting song of the two Birds of Beauty. And sometimes they see the happy pair, flying through a sunlit glade.

# The Three-Pig

Mr. and Mrs. Pig and small Georgie Pig were on their way to visit Grandad Grunter who lived on the other side of the farm.

As they came to the Big Field, they met the Nosey Goat.

"You're not going through the Big Field?" asked the Nosey Goat. "You can't go through there!" The Nosey Goat looked frightened.

"What do you mean?" asked Mrs. Pig. "We always go that way to Grandad Grunter's."

"Not now you can't. Not now that the New Bull is living there," shouted the Nosey Goat. "Haven't you heard? He's not like the Old Bull, you know. He's wild and terrible and chases all the other animals. He tossed two sheep right over the hedge. They had such a fright they're both still in bed!"

"Well," said Mr. Pig firmly, "we're not afraid of the New Bull." He opened the gate and the three pigs entered the Big Field.

The field looked empty and they were halfway to the gate on the other side when they heard an enormous bellow. They turned around. And there, not fifty yards away, was the New Bull.

The New Bull glared at the Pig family. His eyes were round and big and black as coal-shed doors. He was so angry he began to shake all over.

Suddenly he snorted, "Charge!" and lowered his horns.

There was no time for the pigs to escape. The gates were much too far away.

"Quick," said Mr. Pig to small Georgie Pig. "Jump on your mother's back and stand quite still."

Small Georgie Pig did as he was told. Then Mrs. Pig climbed on to Mr. Pig's enormous back and they stood and waited, one on top of the other.

The New Bull stopped short. He couldn't believe his eyes. When he began his charge he thought there were three pigs in his field. Now, at the end of his charge, he found himself looking at a very strange animal indeed. It had three heads, three tails, six eyes, six ears, and legs all over the place.

"Who do you think you are?" demanded the New Bull.

"I'm a Three-Pig," answered Mr. Pig. "Who are you?"

The New Bull was quite upset. No one had dared to answer him back before.

"I . . . I . . . I'm the New Bull," he said.

"You're only a One-Bull," said Mr Pig in a lofty voice. "You're a simple One-Bull and you live in just one field. I'm a Three-Pig and I can go anywhere on the farm."

The New Bull didn't know what to say. The Three-Pig seemed so sure of itself.

"Well, er, yes. If you say so," he replied.

"I do say so," answered Mr. Pig sharply. "And you had better mind your manners, One-Bull. I've heard that you were cruel to the sheep the other day."

"Ermm," said the New Bull. He lowered his head and looked suitably ashamed.

"Yes," said Mr. Pig. "You just watch it. If I hear any more stories like that, I'll tell all the other animals. Even the cows will refuse to speak to you."

"Oh dear," said the New Bull. "I wouldn't like that at all."

And he promised, there and then, to be kind to all the animals on the farm.

"O.K.," said Mr. Pig. "I'm going to see Grandad Grunter now. Goodbye, One-Bull."

"Goodbye, Three-Pig," said the New Bull.

After that, the New Bull became much more friendly. The other animals on the farm were all delighted. Mr. and Mrs. Pig and small Georgie Pig were voted Top Animals of the Month, and they were given a beautiful new carpet to put in their sty.

Stories by the four authors appear on the
following pages:

# Maybe I'll Sleep in the Bathtub Tonight

## and Other Funny Bedtime Poems

by
**Debbie Levy**

Illustrated by
**Stephanie Buscema**

STERLING
New York / London

**For anyone who believes that laughter is the best lullaby**
**—D.L.**

**For my Grandmother Dolores and Grandfather John**
**—S.B.**

STERLING and the distinctive Sterling logo are registered trademarks of Sterling Publishing Co., Inc.

**Library of Congress Cataloging-in-Publication Data**

Levy, Debbie.
Maybe I'll sleep in the bathtub tonight : and other funny bedtime poems/by Debbie Levy;
illustrated by Stephanie Buscema.
p. cm.
ISBN 978-1-4027-4944-5
1. Bedtime--Juvenile poetry. 2. Children's poetry, American. 3. Humorous poetry, American.
I. Buscema, Stephanie, ill. II. Title.

PS3612.E9368M39 2010
811'.6--dc22
2008048826

2 4 6 8 10 9 7 5 3 1
Lot #: 11/09

Published by Sterling Publishing Co., Inc.
387 Park Avenue South, New York, NY 10016
www.sterlingpublishing.com/kids
Text copyright © 2010 by Debbie Levy
Illustrations copyright © 2010 by Stephanie Buscema

Distributed in Canada by Sterling Publishing
c/o Canadian Manda Group, 165 Dufferin Street, Toronto, Ontario, Canada M6K 3H6
Distributed in the United Kingdom by GMC Distribution Services, Castle Place, 166 High Street, Lewes, East Sussex, England BN7 1XU
Distributed in Australia by Capricorn Link (Australia) Pty. Ltd. P.O. Box 704, Windsor, NSW 2756, Australia

**Printed in China**
**All Rights Reserved**

Sterling ISBN 978-1-4027-4944-5

For information about custom editions, special sales, premium and corporate purchases,
please contact Sterling Special Sales Department at 800-805-5489 or specialsales@sterlingpublishing.com.
The artwork was prepared using gouache on water color paper.

Designed by Kate Moll and Lauren Rille

# CONTENTS

# SLEEP TIGHT

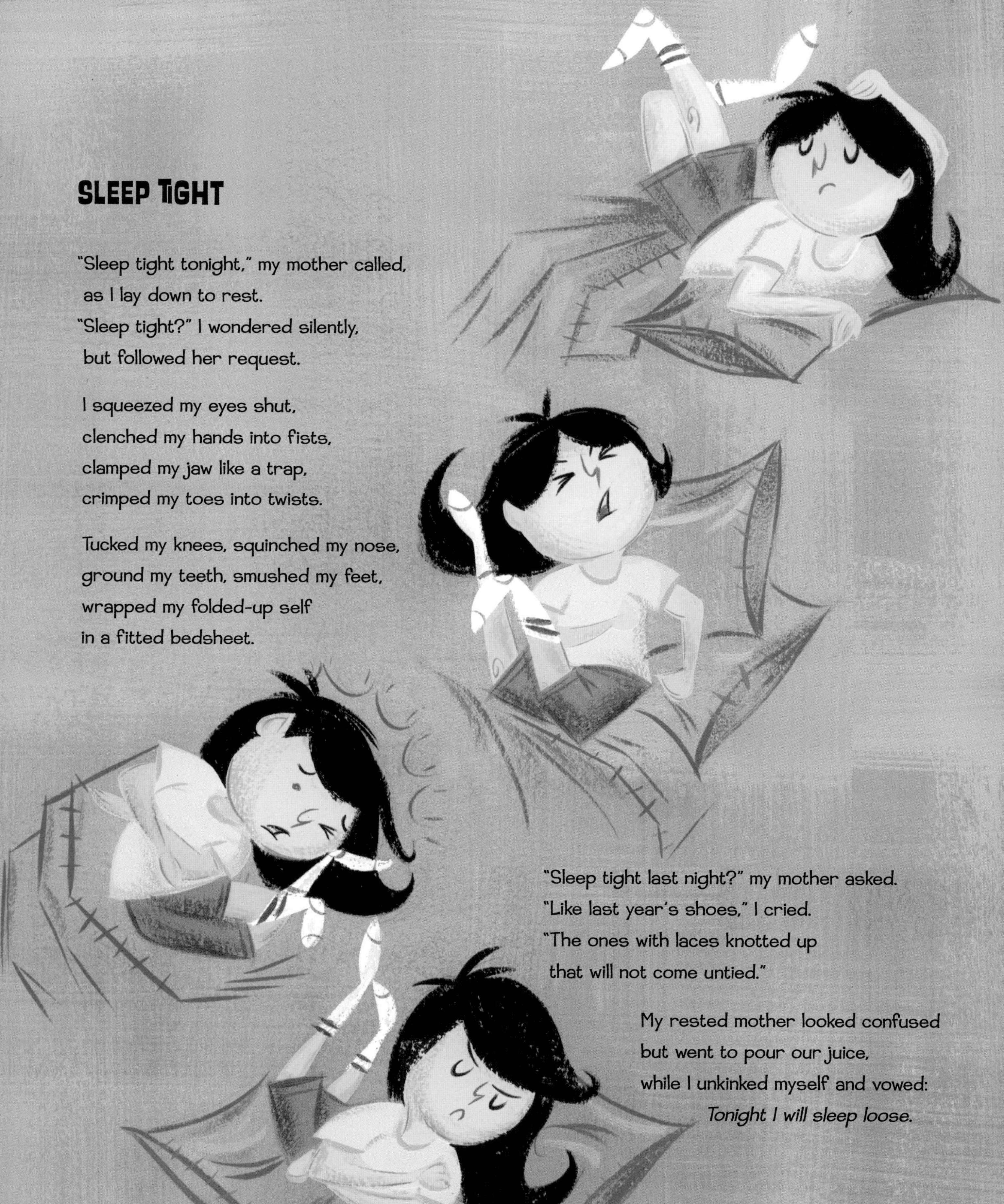

"Sleep tight tonight," my mother called,
 as I lay down to rest.
"Sleep tight?" I wondered silently,
 but followed her request.

I squeezed my eyes shut,
clenched my hands into fists,
clamped my jaw like a trap,
crimped my toes into twists.

Tucked my knees, squinched my nose,
ground my teeth, smushed my feet,
wrapped my folded-up self
in a fitted bedsheet.

"Sleep tight last night?" my mother asked.
"Like last year's shoes," I cried.
"The ones with laces knotted up
 that will not come untied."

My rested mother looked confused
but went to pour our juice,
while I unkinked myself and vowed:
    Tonight I will sleep loose.

# BuNk BED KiNG

Look at him up there,
like some sort of king.
He's on top of the world,
while I'm hunkering
down here in this dungeon,
where I can't even stand
without hitting my head—
and I'd like to demand
why the powers-that-be
(our parents, that is)
said that *this* is my space,
and *that* one is his.
Don't I also deserve
the fresh air up top,
and the wide-open space?
I insist that we swap!
I insist on my turn
to rule over nights.
I insist!

Just as soon as I'm not scared
of heights.

## PILLOW SQUAWK

"One pillow is not enough," the spoiled princess said.
And so they brought another pillow for her royal head.

"Two pillows are much too flat," the princess crossly moaned.
They brought a plumper pillow in, yet still the princess groaned.

"Three pillows are way too few," she scolded angrily.
But four, five, six, and seven did not stop the misery.

"More pillows! I want them now!" the bratty princess called.
Soon every pillow was in her room, but nonetheless she bawled:

"I'll never fall asleep on these! These pillows are the WORST!"
She jumped and flailed and punched and kicked—
and then the pillows burst.

"A-choo, a-choo, a-choo, a-choo, a-choo, a-choo, a-SNEEZE!"
Poor princess.
All those feather pillows gave her allergies.

## NIGHT CLOTHES

Some people sleep with their pants on.
Some people sleep in a shirt.
I wear this rig that's three sizes too big
in case I should have a growth spurt.

## MORE NIGHT CLOTHES

Pete likes to sleep in pajamas.
Gwen slumbers best in a gown.
Shawn goes to bed with a shoe on h s head
for sleepwalking while upside-down.

# SLEEPOVER

"Do you wanna sleep over?" Ted asked Fred.
"Sleep over what?" Fred said.
"My house, of course," Ted replied with a grin.
Fred looked at Ted with dread.

"Are you sure?" Fred asked with fear in his voice.
"Your house is quite tall, you know.
  Once we climb up there and over the top,
  what if the wind starts to blow?"

"And if you want to sleep *under* your house,
that would be dangerous, too.
There are snakes down there, and bugs everywhere.
What if they bite me or you?"

"So here's what I'm thinking. I hope you'll agree.
Here's what we'll do," Fred said.
"We won't sleep over or under your house—
We'll sleep *inside* it instead."

Ted just sat there.
He tried to be kind.
"Hey, Fred," he said.
"Never mind."

# TWO TIMES BOO

Trina and Trish,
  identical twins,
  share a room,
  a bed,
  the blanket,
  a sheet,
  the pillow,
  a thumb
(now *there's* a real treat!).

The twins also share
  a fear of the dark,
  and so,
  when they turn out the light,
  Trish keeps her left eye
  stretched open real wide,
  while Trina keeps open
  her right.

10

## MY CLOSET

There's nothing in my closet,
just shirts and coats and shoes.
There's nothing more unusual
to stop me from my snooze.

There's no one hiding way behind
the boxes on the floor.
That hissing sound is not some creature
blowing down the door.

I don't hear something sharpening
its claws against the wall,
about to pounce upon some prey—
like me!—it plans to maul.

There's nothing in my closet,
just shirts and coats—*WHAT'S THAT?!*
Oh. Like I said, there's nothing there,
unless you count my cat.

## THUMB-THING NEW

For seven years, Tom went to sleep while sucking his left thumb,
until one day he broke it in the school gymnasium.
His bandaged finger was no good for sucking, so he tried
to use his right thumb as a sub, but wasn't satisfied.
Tom always knew this baby habit was something he'd outgrow!
(He falls asleep now, happily, while sucking his left toe.)

12

## MAYBE I'LL SLEEP IN THE BATHTUB TONIGHT

Maybe I'll sleep in the bathtub tonight.
It's not because I'm dirty.
No! The reason why
is so when I
wake up at seven thirty
I won't forget to take a bath,
as I forgot today;
as I forgot all week, all month—
in fact, it's been since May.
And since today is August first,
that's ninety days in all.
I don't really think
there's much of a stink—
but my skin is beginning to crawl.
So, yes, I'll sleep in the bathtub tonight,
and yes, I'll try to remember
to wash my slightly cruddy self
sometime before September.

*(In case you're wondering*
*why I don't jump*
*in the shower right now, to de-grime—*
*Really, I would but*
*I'm all tuckered out*
*from writing this bathtubby rhyme.)*

# NIGHT SWIMMING

I knew that Sally could not swim,
I saw it in her eyes.
But she's the kind who won't say no.
She's the kind who tries.

That night when I told Sally that
the water seemed too rough,
she tossed her head as if to say,
"I'm made of tougher stuff."

The roar of waves was deafening.
The fishes gasped for breath.
The crabs and other sea life—
well, some met an early death.

14

Our boat lurched in the churning surf.
I held fast to my seat.
And in the moonlight, there was Sally:
She was on her feet.

"Sit down, you fool!" I cried in fear.
"Sit down before you drown!"
But in her eyes I saw that look,
that stubborn, willful frown. . . .

Perhaps I could have saved her
from the water's awful wrath.
Instead I sat there yelling out:

"MY DOLL FELL IN THE BATH!"

## FLOATING AWAY

Just *one* sip of water, just *one* tiny drink,
just *one* taste and I'll go to sleep in a wink.

*Aah . . .*
Oh, *two* sips, I beg you—my lips are so dry,
my mouth is a desert, so please, liquefy!

*Aah . . .*
If only you'd fill the cup up to the top
I'd take *three* big gulps and my pleading would stop.

*Aah . . .*
This *fourth* glass of water is just what I need. . . .
I'm sleepy . . . good night now . . .

. . . OH, NO, MOM, I PEED!

## SNACK ATTACK

Essie liked to eat in bed.
Food tasted better there.
In bed she ate things she refused
when in a kitchen chair.

Like beets and beans
and canned sardines,
roasted trout and sauerkraut,
pickled eel with lemon peel,
liver stew on honeydew.

Yes, Essie loved her bedtime feasts,
but they came to a halt
the night an ant politely whispered,
"Please, miss—pass the salt."

## LULLABY-BYE

Rock-a-bye, baby,
on the tree top,
you know the rest—
that baby goes plop.
Did people really
stick babies in trees?
This song is a nightmare!
Next lullaby, please.

## CREATURE COMFORTS

My dog lies on my feet.
My cat lies on my face.
My rabbit, ferret, hamster,
    lizard—each is in its place.
My turtle's fast asleep.
My goldfish is awake.
My snake is coiled around my neck—
Wait. I *have* no snake.

18

## THE CRICKET

"Chirp, chirp, chirp," the cricket chirped.
I thought it sounded cute.
Chirp-chirp-chirp-chirp-chirp-chirp-chirp.
Okay. Enough. Now scoot!

It didn't scoot, I couldn't sleep;
neither could Chester, my cat.
I nudged Chester off the bed and said,
"Go put an end to that."

Chester pounced, and I called out,
"Swat it, Chester, swat it!"
I cheered my cat, for in the dark,
I thought that he had got it.

Chester got the cricket, yes—
it jumped into his mouth,
and didn't stop, but hopped inside of
Chester, heading south.

Once the cricket reached his belly,
Chester gave a burp,
and ever since, when Chester purrs,
he goes: "Chirp, chirp, chirp, chirp."

19

## SWEET DREAMS

*Sweet dreams.*
Why, thank you, that sounds very nice.
I'll doze off to visions of sugar and spice. . . .

I would love to dream about cookies, but then
my brother will find out and want to eat ten.
All night long he'll be pleading,
and that's not what I'm needing,
so I think I won't dream about cookies.

If my dreams turn to chocolate, I'll get no relief,
since my mother is known as a cocoa-bean thief.
With her fudge-crazy craving,
she'll be ranting and raving,
so I think I won't dream about chocolate.

My sister's completely obsessed over gummies.
She eats them as if she's got seventeen tummies.
If I'm happily chewing,
she'll be *aahing* and *oohing*,
so I think I won't dream about gummies.

But if I resist all these claims on my treats,
and if I keep to myself all these sweets,
then I'll gorge on a pound of
a super-sized mound of
an all-night dessert, so
my stomach will hurt—oh!
I'll get hyper from feeding
on the sugar I'm eating.

I'll be such a wreck! I'll be up every hour.
So thanks very much—
I will keep my dreams sour.

# LOOK WHO'S SLEEPING

Won't you please sit with me here in my room?
If you stay, I will fall asleep better.
You don't have to sing or to read or to talk,
not a sentence, a word, or a letter.

In just a few minutes, I'll be deep in my dreams.
You'll get back to the work you're ignoring—
Um.
I hate to disturb you.
I'm happy you're here—
but shouldn't *I* be the one who is snoring?

# PUCKER UP

In the movies, when people wake up in the morning,
they kiss one another without any warning.

Don't believe it! Remember, those people are fake!
You know what your mouth tastes like when you awake.

It's curdled and clotted like milk that has rotted
when you leave it outside in the heat.
Like the dog when he licks a mysterious mix
of old garbage that used to be . . . meat.

So please don't be fooled by those actors on-screen
who lock lips together before they are clean—

In real life, a kiss with such odious breath
belongs in a horror film:

## THE KISS OF DEATH

23

## AM I?

I am not tired.

Not a bit, not a dab, not a drop, not a mite.

I am not tired tonight.

### Am not tired!

Not a speck, not a spot, not a crumb, not a jot.

Do you hear me?

I am not.

## Not tired.

Not a grain, not a mote, not an inch, not a gram.

I am wide awake. I am . . .

Tired.